BUOYGEIST

BY

TOM RIMER

SHADOW SPARK PUBLISHING

BOUYGEIST

To my oldest friends,
Scott Frye & Kevin Hayes

Think of me and I will wake.
Find me and I will ready.
Call me and I will listen.
Want me and I will come.
Need of me and I will bleed...
...of you.

PROLOGUE

1978

PLAY ▷

Ten Years *Before*

CATHUNK, CATHUNK, CATHUNK, CATHUNK.

That was what the waves sounded like, rhythmically crashing into the underside of Jerry's aluminum rowboat. It was dark, well after midnight, and he permitted the murkiness to cloak the agony unconsciously displayed across his face. His head rested on top of his reddened knees, which he clasped tightly to his chest. Two lights, the jaundiced bulb above the door to the Harbormaster's office and the effulgent moon, were his only sources of illumination. Their combined gaze lingered over him intrusively, and he burrowed his head even further between his legs.

Jerry was alone in the middle of the marina. At that hour, there weren't any signs of life—not even a flickering flashlight or someone up and using the bathroom in the cabin of their docked schooner. He was completely isolated, in his little dingy, out on the water. Which is exactly how he wanted it.

A single tear rolled down his cheek, but he made no attempt to wipe it away. Jerry reached for the small, black transistor radio resting near his feet—which were sheathed in his wrinkled, leather boat shoes—and flicked it on. A sad saxophone solo—the bridge to a song he couldn't identify—greeted him. It seemed appropriate for the moment, and he didn't care to surf for another option, so he let the soloist play on.

It's already done, Jerry. What does it even matter?

He sniffed. It was true. He was out in the middle of the creek for a reason.

Jerry closed his eyes.

I'm just so tired of this. Everything.

He took a deep breath of the marshy tide before exhaling, sending it all back.

And then, Jerry opened his eyes.

It was darker. Darker than before. At first, he thought it was just his eyes readjusting and that his night vision had yet to kick back in. But—

No. No, it's not that.

He could still see the tiny light over the small shack back on land, but the added brightness provided by the moon was gone. Something was blocking it out. Something massive.

Jerry took a deep breath. He held it for a long time in his lungs, savoring the feeling for a moment, and then nodded.

"So, it's true," he said aloud, his body beginning to shake involuntarily as he realized what was behind him. "Now, I know. Now, I finally know."

Drip, drip, drip, drip.

The sound was clear. Just over his shoulder. Beyond the bow of his rowboat. Rivulets of evil pouring into the water, off of something substantial enough to block out the protective, consolatory light of the moon.

Drip, drip, drip, drip.

Jerry tried to gather enough saliva in his mouth to swallow but found that to be an impossibility. He wanted to turn around and face what he knew was hovering there, but was also too overwrought and stricken by the terror coursing through his extremities to make himself do so. The car keys in his pocket started to jingle in grim synchronization with the tremor that rippled uncontrollably through his body, and—at the very same moment—the saxophonist on the radio reached a crescendo in his well-timed performance.

Drip, drip, drip, drip.

Fear constricted itself like a serpent around his chest, and Jerry found himself struggling to breathe. "I-I-I-I'm not going to turn around. I'm s-sorry. I shouldn't have done this. This was a mistake. I-I've changed my mind and—"

Jerry felt the warm spurt fall on his bare legs before he realized where the sensation was coming from and before he recognized the large metal object protruding from his gut as the endblade of a throwing harpoon.

You did this to yourself, Jerry.

He tried to speak, but more blood flowed out past his lips and teeth. Jerry turned then, wide-eyed, to greet his assailant and screamed as he finally laid eyes on the figure floating three feet above the darkened surface of Cape Cod's murderous, unsympathetic, unrelenting waters.

CHAPTER ONE

MILTY BURKITTS

PLAY ▷

Bay Video

EVIL HAS A WAY of finding the cracks. The little crevices that splinter through life and leave imperfections on the otherwise perfect. They are fractures that widen just enough to allow pollution and corruption to run wild, to wreak havoc, and sully even the things that make us most whole, most happy, and undeniably most human. Some folks, stewards of good, are tasked with shielding our most treasured artifacts from the smear that so easily rots. Unknowingly they—bulwarks against the unending, crushing waves of vile, putrid sea—are all that stand between us and the evil erosion. The sands of time gradually wash away and extinguish all that we know and hold most dear, and would do so even more quickly if not for the bastions, the protectors, and the keepers.

Milty Burkitts was one of those keepers.

A caretaker.

A bulwark.

He didn't know it yet, of course, but he was just the same.

Crack.

Milty stared down at the crushed, pitiful specimen lying helplessly at his feet. Bending his knees, he sighed. Squatting over the broken carcass, he began to collect the pieces and shards that'd been kicked haphazardly about.

"This is madness," he said through gritted teeth. "I mean, why? *Why*? What's the point of this? It just can't—it can't keep happening." He stood gingerly, cradling the ruin dangling from his fingertips. "We need to do something about this, Surge."

Sergio "Surge" Garcia, owner of Bay Video, held out a broom and waited for his employee to take it from him. "And what *something* do you expect me to do about it, Son? You think I can afford to install security cameras here to catch these little pissants?"

"But, Surge—"

"But, *nuthin'*." He took a deep breath and then dragged the back of a massive hand over the sweat beading at the tip of his nose. "Look, Milty, do you even know what you're holding there in your hands? I'm serious. Take a good long gander. Just look at it. Tell me what you see. Hmm? What is that? Be specific."

Milty looked down at the mangled, black, plastic rectangle in his hands. "It's, uh—"

"It's not goddamn rocket science. What *is* it?"

"—it's a VHS tape?"

"Mhmmm. Of?"

"Of? It's—I, uh—"

"Well? Come on, then. Don't pretend you don't know this stuff like the back of your hand. Acting like you haven't seen it before. For chrissakes, Milton. Just read the damn title."

"—it's, uh, *Sleepover Slasher Massacre III: Pillow Fight*."

Surge nodded. "Exactly. And you wanna know exactly how many people have rented that trash in recent memory?"

"Uh, I mean—"

"Ha! Exactly. None. Nada. Precisely zero." He sighed. "Who gives a rat's ass that this waste of shelf space got stepped on tonight? Certainly not me. And you shouldn't either. No one's gonna miss it. Not for a nanosecond. Was gonna throw that in the freebie bin next week anyway." He took a step closer to the crime scene before adjusting the red, sweat-stained bandana strapped across his forehead. "I keep tellin' you. We need to be makin' room for all the new stuff. It's what my customers want. *Not* this junk."

Milty took another long look at the mess in his hands before throwing it into an uncovered aluminum garbage can. "I guess so,

Surge. But, you know, it's not the first time this kind of thing has happened. These kids come in here and have no respect for your business. I'm just looking out for you."

Surge threw a bulging forearm over Milty's shoulders. "I appreciate you, Kid. I mean it. You're one of the good ones. There are too few of you out in the world. But, Man, this is *life*. You think I got to be one of the only black business owners on the Lower Cape by picking fights where fights need not be picked? 'Course not. You've got to know when it's time and when it's not time. Capeesh? And that's not to say there aren't causes worth going to battle for. I've thrown plenty of punches in my day, but only when I needed to. *Only then*. This—" he pointed at a few straggling pieces of plastic at his feet. "This ain't worth it."

Milty nodded. "Alright, Surge. If you say so. You're the boss."

Surge's laugh bellowed through the empty video rental store. "You're damn right I am. And don't you forget it. Now," his expression turned more serious and he furrowed his massive gray eyebrows. "Sweep that shit up. It's closing time."

Milty stuck his thumb out in the affirmative and then got to work. He focused his attention on a few pieces of popcorn dropped in an aisle that currently housed all their action movies. A cardboard cutout of Arnold Schwarzenegger from *Commando* stared, judging him at the end of the row.

"What, you think you could do better, Arnie?"

On cue, from the opposite side of the store, Surge hollered through a laugh. "Stop talking to my promotional materials! I'm paying you to clean, not to gab with that stiff!"

Milty finished tidying the aisle before responding. "Woah, woah. Hey now. That *stiff* is only the greatest action movie star of my generation. I swear, it's just a matter of time before he gets an Oscar nom. Any day now. Just you wait."

Somewhere, barely audible over the sound of Surge cleaning out the cash register, Milty heard the man mumble, "Strap in, Son. We're gonna be waiting a lifetime for that fantasy."

Milty laughed to himself and finished his walk-through of the store. The storage closet was open and he tossed his broom inside. It clanged against a back wall and he winced, half expecting Surge to lecture him about being more careful with company property. When no admonishment came, he shrugged and stretched his skinny pale arms behind his head until his shoulders cracked. Yawning, he approached the front counter and dropped onto his elbows. Surge didn't look up from counting his money but spoke with sincere interest and somehow without appearing to lose his place.

"Plans tonight? That was an awful quick clean up."

Milty shook his head. "No. I mean, it's Thursday night. Gotta be back in bright and early tomorrow."

Surge continued his count. "Hasn't stopped you before. I know what you do on Thursday nights." He lifted an eyebrow momentarily and then returned to his task.

Milty cleared his throat. "Oh, you mean the Drive-In?"

Surge nodded.

"Well, yeah—but probably not tonight. I'm kinda tired."

Surge laughed. "Suit yourself. Just hate to see you not getting out more often. There's an entire world out there, and that Diane—"

"Diane and I are just friends, Surge. *Friends*. I've told you this. Many, many times."

Surge slammed the cash register door shut. "That you have. And I've told you I think that girl likes you. Man, I'm just sayin'—"

Milty glared at him, and the shop owner put his hands in the air defensively. "Alright, alright. I get it, I get it. I know when to give up." He paused for a moment, considering something as he reached for his jacket. "Wait. *Wait*. I know what's up. I'm no fool." He wagged a finger at Milty. "Oh, ho, ho. You sly devil."

Milty took a step toward the door and grabbed his neon green trucker hat from its hanger. It read, simply, **EASTHAM** in electric blue font. "What?" he droned, feigning ignorance.

"I know what's goin' down." Surge continued. "Ha! That other girl, the one you've been pining over since you graduated four years ago. This is the weekend she comes home. Right? Homecoming, isn't it?"

Milty started to push open the front door, but Surge reached over his head and slammed it shut. "Surge, it's not like that."

"Like hell, it isn't."

"It's not. I promise."

Surge's frame impressively dwarfed that of his employee. Still, he had somehow managed to squeeze his way into the tiny space Milty'd left between himself and the glass exit. "So, let me just get this straight—"

"And then you'll let me go?"

"—and then I'll let you go."

Milty rolled his eyes. "Okay."

Surge stared down at his protégé. "So, ha—so just *coincidentally*, you decide you're not gonna hang with, uh—"

"Diane."

"—*Diane* tonight at the Drive-In. Like you do every *other* Thursday night. And just *coincidentally*, of course, this is the same weekend, uh—"

"Velma."

"Right, *Velma*. You bail on Diane the same weekend Velma," he pretended to check an imaginary notepad on his palm, "Returns to Eastham for the first time in, oh... four years? That's what you told me last week, right? Hasn't been back since you all graduated?"

Milty nodded. "Yes."

"Ha! Coincidence? Not buyin' it. Nuh uh. No way. That's some grade-A bullshit and you know it."

Milty pushed past him out the door and Surge didn't stop him. "I told you it's—it's *complicated*."

Behind him, Surge flicked off the lights. Keys jingled into the night air, signaling he was finally locking up. "Complicated? Oh, it's *complicated*, is it? And how's that? Seems pretty goddamned straightforward to me—"

"She's bringing her boyfriend, Surge." Milty waited until the new information had sunk far enough into the other man's brain that understanding finally appeared visibly on his face. "They've been dating for a while now, I think."

Surge straddled up beside him and gave Milty a paternal pat on the back. For a moment, the two just walked quietly into the parking lot. "Well, shoot. Sorry to hear that, Kid. But, if you ask me—and I know you're not—but, if you *did* ask me, I'd tell ya it's probably time to move on. She never did give the time of day to you in high school and there's no reason she's going to—"

Milty separated and turned to face him. "Trust me, *I know*, I know. This is why I said… it's not like that. I'm not planning to try to find her, and I have no crazy notion that anything's changed. But, it's just—all those feelings are getting drudged up again. That's all. And I didn't wanna go to the Drive-In tonight because—well, I guess I just needed a night off."

Surge squinted at him. "And you were worried you might run into Velma there."

That wasn't even a question.

Milty pursed his lips. "Maybe?"

Surge sighed. "Can't run from this stuff your entire life, Kid. Gotta face these things head-on. If you ask me—"

"I didn't."

"Yeah, but—if you did—I'd tell you it's better to rip the damn band-aid clean off. Get it over with. Get *seeing* her over with, I mean. And then, who knows, maybe you can give this Diane or…I dunno, someone else a chance."

Milty looked up at him. There was a warmth coming off of the man. Spider-webs cracked from the corners of his large brown eyes, and his smile, to the impressionable twenty-something, was the most comforting sight in the world right then. The kid pushed the brim of his foam cap a bit higher so that his eyes and his genuine appreciation could be fully seen. "Thanks, Surge. I'll think on it."

The two waved at each other and walked in their separate directions. Though the autumnal chill that night was expected, somehow it felt even colder than the harsh wind off of Cape Cod Bay should have dictated that early in October. Milty took a deep breath of the salty air, bowed his head, and let the darkness of the poorly illuminated street carry him homeward.

CHAPTER TWO

MILTY BURKITTS

PLAY ▷

19 Clamneck Circle

MILTY SHUT THE FRONT door behind him but did not lock it. They lived in a relatively safe town with a minimal amount of criminal tomfoolery, and break-ins were almost nonexistent. Besides being unnecessary, simply turning a latch was, more than anything, a few steps beyond the scope of what the shaggy-haired daydreamer had the energy for on that particular evening.

What're they even gonna steal? Mom's Tom Jones 8-tracks?

There was a clinking sound in the other room. Forks and knives attacking porcelain dishware. His family was already at the dinner table.

"Milty?" a mouthful of red meat—*I can only assume*—called to him. "Home at last?"

He threw his hat on the couch before anyone had a chance to ask him to remove it. "No, it's Sally Struthers."

This caused his father to guffaw far more loudly than was expected or necessary, given the rather lame attempt at a joke. "Well, get in here, *Sally*. Burgers tonight."

Milty crossed the living room into the adjoining dining area. It wasn't a full dining room, per se, but rather a table that shared a not-too-distant space with their couch and TV console. He sat down in the only empty chair, dinner already waiting for him, and registered no shock as his father sawed away at his own meal. *Every*

Thursday night at the Burkitt residence was Burger Night, and *every* Thursday night was also when Marv Burkitt ate his burger with a knife and fork like a goddamned psycho.

"How was work?" His mother didn't bother to look up from her meal, and Milty couldn't tell if she was listening or even cared for a response. She took a long drag of a cigarette and tapped it into her favorite brown-glass ashtray before he was able to open his mouth.

"Same as ever. Nothing new to report."

His mother, Lorraine, took another drag. "Hmm," was all she said.

Marv Burkitts cut too deeply with his knife and they were all rewarded with an ear-splitting screech. Everyone else cringed, but he seemed not to notice. "Eloise has got plans tonight. Eh, Eloise? You tell Milty 'bout those plans yet? Why don't you go ahead and tell him?" A blob of yellow-red, ketchup-mustard mix dribbled down the man's chin as he grinned like a Jack-o-lantern that'd just bitten into a puss-filled slug.

Eloise turned her head slowly to Milty and blinked twice. "I've got plans tonight."

Milty looked to his younger sister as he took his first bite of dinner. "Oh yeah?" he said, dabbing at the corner of his mouth with a napkin. "What kinda plans?"

Eloise blinked a couple more times at him, as if responding was completely zapping her of all her strength. "Going to the mall with Toni to...walk...around the mall."

Milty swallowed. "Nice. Sounds like a fun time."

Marv Burkitts leaned forward. "It does, doesn't it? Hey, Milty, I don't mean to be a nudge, but—"

"Dad."

"—but, oh I dunno, I was wondering why *you* don't ever, ya know, make plans. Of your own. With any of *your* friends. You really should think about—"

"Dad."

"—making plans. You know, when I was your age—"

"Dad."

Lorraine tapped the stub of her cigarette again. "Marv, leave him alone."

"—I was *always* out. Like, every stinkin' night. Me and the boys. Top down on the T-Bird, picking up chicks—"

"Dad."

"Ew, gross."

"Marv, leave him alone."

"—doing donuts in the high school parking lot. The Stones singin' in our ears, and the wind blowin' through our hairs. I'm just sayin', I think you need to do more of that. Live your life. As my father always used to remind me, 'You only get one—'"

"DAD!"

Marv finally looked up and snapped out of his trance. "Uh, yeah? What's the matter? I say something wrong? What'd I say?"

Milty pushed his seat away from the table, stood up, and took his plate with him. "I'm gonna go eat in my room." He walked toward the basement door and, just before descending, heard his dad mumble something that sounded like, "—such a sensitive guy, huh? You know, when I was his age, we could take criticism, and we respected the wisdom our elders had to impart on us and—"

Milty slammed the door behind him, not wanting to hear the rest of what the man had to say. He took the wooden stairs two at a time and they creaked under his weight. Entering his basement lair, which a few years before had been bequeathed by his parents in a lackluster bribe to tempt him to live at home a bit longer, he plopped down into an old, cat-clawed recliner. It was a relic from Milty's childhood, rescued when his dad had tried—unsuccessfully—to put it out on the curb. He swung the leg-rest up and quickly devoured the remainder of his burger. When finished, he let the plate balance on his belly as he took in the comforting sight of his dwelling.

My place. All mine.

Surrounding him were cardboard cutouts of film icons and shelves of once-played-with action figures, now proudly displayed in places of honor. Most distinctly, were the mildewed movie posters that covered nearly every inch of the basement walls. An added perk of working at Bay Video, besides the measly $3.35 an hour that he took home, was that Surge allowed him first dibs on all the promo stuff before he either sold it or tossed it into the dumpster. To Milty, these "bonuses" made his job, at least in part, worth all the hassle.

His most treasured piece was a small cardboard cutout of Gizmo from the movie *Gremlins* (which he'd perched on top of his prized VCR) and an *Indiana Jones and the Temple of Doom* poster that he'd plastered prominently behind his battered loveseat (another family heirloom that his father the lunatic had attempted to discard).

It's good to have friends.

Milty closed his eyes. Though he would never admit it out loud, his father was right. He *did* need to get out more. The problem was that this weekend, in particular, it just felt safer for him to hide out in his dungeon. *She* was coming home after all, and the last thing Milty wanted *her* to see—or for him to have to explain—was that he was still working at the video rental place...the same one he'd worked at years earlier, long before they'd graduated from high school. While everyone else was off growing up and starting their lives, Milty was still doing his best to hide from adulthood.

Besides, he thought, *she's bringing him.*

She, of course, was Velma Green. Word on the street was that she was bringing her new boyfriend (the local gossip always managed to find its way back to Bay Video) with plans of showing him the hotspots of her hometown, introducing the guy to all her old friends, and generally just being *around* for a few days.

Yeah, no. I'm good. Happy to miss out on all of that.

Without moving from his chair, Milty reached toward the bookshelf beside him and pulled out his senior yearbook. He casually flipped a few pages, though knew exactly what part of the book he was headed for. Quickly, he located Velma's picture. Just as they always had, her curly blond locks hung in front of her large green eyes, and her smile seemingly stretched across the entire frame. Her senior quote was a line from the movie *Footloose*:

"Hey, hey! What's this I see? I thought this was a party. LET'S DANCE!"

Milty slammed the book shut. "Ugh, how I wish." He let his head flop backward and stared up at the drop ceiling, noticing yet another new water stain that he'd definitely need to tell his dad about. The brownish blob vaguely looked like a smiley face, and Milty groaned at it.

"You know what?" he said to the air. "To hell with this. Dad's right." He laughed and pulled on his gray windbreaker. "God love him, the asshole's right. I need to get the hell outta here."

He looked toward the clock on his wall.

It's early enough. I could probably still hit the Drive-In. Sneak up to my usual spot before the movie starts. Get a move on, Kid.

He zippered his jacket and put a foot on the staircase.

And who knows, maybe you'll run into someone. Time to stop being such a downer. Your life—she's awaitin'.

Milty nodded, appreciative of the affirming voice that'd decided to manifest right then. He hurried up the staircase, exited the basement, and sprinted straight for the front door. As the nighttime reacted to his unexpected arrival and an owl hooted an astonished "Well, wouldya look at that", Milty thought he heard his dad call out to him—through another mouth of ground meat and over a bit of disharmonic squealing from sterling silver utensils—"Dat's mumff boy!"

CHAPTER THREE

DIANE SHAW

PLAY ▷

The Drive-In

THE MOVIE WAS *PUMPKINHEAD*. Diane Shaw tried to steal a peek as the opening credits rolled, while loading up the man's jumbo popcorn tub for what was—*already*—the third time.

I get that these are free refills but holy shit man have some self-respect.

She pushed the bucket across the counter and, instead of thanking her, the man shoved a buttery paw of the snack food into his already open, waiting mouth. As he departed, returning to his vehicle, Diane propped herself up on her elbows and settled in to enjoy a bit of the movie before the next customer arrived. Fortunately, it was a Thursday night and Thursday nights were notoriously slow. Not only that, but *Pumpkinhead* had been showing already for a few weeks, and ticket sales hadn't been all that great. In fact, she'd already watched the cheesy monster movie in its entirety at least seven times thanks to the quiet crowds.

So bad it's good, she thought. *So bad it is good.*

Diane loved horror movies and readjusted her black Elvira t-shirt. One of her favorite aspects of her job was that the owner let her wear whatever she wanted, probably because it was dark out and no one could really see her anyway. She *was* sporting a nifty blue Drive-In hat, but that was mostly because she had gnarly beach hair and hadn't found time that evening to shower. It was her regular pattern to surf right up until her shift, often even missing dinner as a result. But she didn't mind. Surfing and movies. Movies and surfing. What else mattered?

Her gaze shifted momentarily and she saw what she so often saw on Thursday evenings.

Milty.

Milty Burkitts. Sitting alone on a hill just beyond the parking lot. On those nights, the Drive-In was understaffed—other than Diane it was only the guy taking tickets at the front gate and the projectionist—and Milty had sagely figured out years ago that no one would pay him any mind if he just hunkered down in the shadows and not-so-covertly watched movies from across the street with his binoculars. For free.

Diane smiled.

And why the hell not? Who's he bothering?

The answer was "no one" and, besides that, he was—

Cute.

She sighed and then realized, face in hands, that she'd been very obviously staring in his direction. His binoculars were still focused on the movie—

So, no harm done.

—but, as she turned around, Diane realized a small line had materialized at the concession stand and a few customers grumbled their greasy annoyances at the minuscule delay they'd been forced to endure. With a meek squeak and a half-hearted apology, she hurried to fill their orders and take their cash. Most of the people in line and at the movie theater on a Thursday night were *year-rounders*. During the summer months, tourists invaded the Drive-In with their neon lawn chairs, aloe-vera-ed sunburns, and bellies filled of overpriced lobster rolls—the vestiges of which often stained their polo shirts and left fishy smells in their too-perfectly manicured beards. Diane preferred the fall, when she knew everyone and the place was quieter, but also had to be on her best behavior because so many of the Drive-In customers that time of year were her mom's friends or her dad's cousin's neighbor, or—worst of all—her former teachers. She finished the few orders and then, when she was fairly certain no one was looking, turned her attention back to Milty. If anyone could draw her focus away from *Pumpkinhead*, it would be that curly-haired *hunk*.

She sighed.

But not too loudly.

Not so loudly that anyone could hear.

I think.

Milty was reaching into a bag of something. Diane squinted. Fries, she thought. From The Fry Fry.

Nom nom.

She licked her lips and checked to make sure neither of the other two employees were nearby.

And why would they be? She snuck a glance at her special edition *Friday the 13th* wristwatch. *Both of those duds are usually snoozing by now.*

She shrugged and threw her legs over the counter. There were no customers headed toward the concession stand and, before that reality could change, she sprinted across the parking lot.

I'll be right back. They'll never even miss me.

When she got to the road, there was no need for her to wait for a safe moment to cross. It was a Thursday night in October. Eastham was a ghost town.

Damn, wouldn't that be nice? A few ghouls haunting this place might even spice things up a bit.

Diane covered the stretch of blacktop in exactly five steps.

Just like always.

When she got to the bottom of the hill, she paused, checked to make sure she didn't have any butter stains on her shirt, and then smoothed her red ponytail where it hung out the back of her Drive-In cap.

Come on, Diane.

She looked toward the top of the hill.

Tonight's gonna be different. I can feel it.

Milty still hadn't noticed her. Or, at least, Diane *thought* he hadn't noticed her. His binoculars remained fixed on the movie screen and his typical MO was to not give up any clues as to what he thought of her or, perhaps more accurately, *if* he had any actual thoughts about her at all. They were friends, sure—or at least Diane believed them to be—but, with Milty, despite her regular attempts to flirt with him, it was hard to really know if she'd even yet appeared as a tiny blip on his oblivious radar.

If he even has a radar.

Not wanting to scare the guy by suddenly materializing out of the shadows, she called up to him.

"See anything you like?"

Milty looked away from his binoculars just long enough to gather who was speaking to him and then returned them to his eyes. "Oh, hey, Diane. Yeah, great movie. Lance Henriksen is so wildly underrated."

Diane climbed the hill. "Yeah," she said. "He's pretty great. Don't murder me, but I think I actually like him more in this movie than in *Aliens*." Milty grunted and she decided to accept the guttural utterance as some sort of tepid agreement. When he said nothing further, she continued. "You know, I thought I might find you up here."

Dumb, Diane. Of course, you'd find him up here. He's always here. Same time, same place.

Milty reached for a fry. "Yeah, well. Thursday night."

Dumb.

"Yeah," Diane said. She waited for an offer to sit or for him to ask about—well, anything—but he didn't. His focus was instead entirely on Stan Winston's grotesque creation. She cleared her throat, deciding not to wait for an invitation that would never come. "Uh, mind if I join you?"

Milty nodded and held out the bag of fries. Diane reached in and snagged a few as she lowered herself to the ground beside him. "Hey, thanks, man."

So smooth.

Again, he grunted at her. "By the way, aren't you supposed to be at work?"

She turned to face him. "You say that every time I come up here. The answer is always the same. Who's gonna notice either way?"

Milty turned his binoculars toward the concession stand. "You're right. No one's waiting at your counter."

Diane sighed. Their scripted interaction happened in much the same way each time she paid him a visit on his hill. He always asked the same questions. She gave the same answers. And there was never anyone waiting for her to return.

She chewed the corner of her lip and looked toward the screen.

Say it.

Diane rolled her eyes at herself as she fiddled with a neon green shoelace.

Ask him.

She cracked her knuckles, waiting for the right moment. She wanted his full attention but there happened to be a particularly important scene in the movie currently playing out in front of them. She only had a few seconds before his ability to concentrate on anything else would be fully lost for the evening.

Just do it before—

"Hey, Diane?" he said, surprising her. She turned and realized he was looking at her. Actually, facing her.

Caught off guard, she stumbled over her words. "Uh—I mean—um, yeah? What, uh—?"

Oh my God. Is this it? Is he actually, FINALLY, going to ask you? Get a hold of yourself, Diane.

"Do you—?"

She sat up straighter and brushed invisible crumbs off of her Elvira t-shirt. "Yes?"

"I mean—I—well—"

He's going to say it.

"What's up, Milty?"

He gulped. "Okay, don't get mad—"

"Promise I won't."

"—But I, *personally*—"

"Yeah?"

She watched him swallow a bunch of spit. He was gearing up for something big.

"—don't think this movie is really deserving of a sequel."

Diane groaned and dramatically flopped back down on the ground. Unable to help herself, she spat, "That's *it*?"

He was still distracted by the movie, but she could see his brow furrow. "What's *it*? What do you m—"

"Never mind," she said through clenched teeth. "Just—never mind."

Milty did pick up on the tone of her voice then and leaned down on his elbow beside her. "I'm sorry. I shouldn't have said that. That was—"

"No, it's ok."

"—insensitive. I know how much you like this movie. I just—"

"Really, it's not a big deal."

"—think this is great as its own thing. As a stand-alone. Ya know?"

"Yah, I know. *I know*, Milty. It's fine. I promise."

He nodded. "Okay." He looked back into his field glasses toward the Drive-In. "Oh, hey, looks like you've got a little line forming now after all."

Diane leapt to her feet. "Shit. Shit, shit, shit. Okay, well—"

"You gotta go."

"Yeah." She started back down the hill. She'd almost made it back to the street when Milty called out to her. "I'm sorry!"

Diane stopped in her tracks and spun around, an idea blossoming suddenly. She couldn't help herself. "Hey, you wanna make it up to me? Like, *for real*?"

Milty tilted his head, perhaps unsure where their conversation—or her incoming proposition—was going. "How?"

She cupped both of her hands around her mouth to make certain she was heard clearly. "Come to the bonfire with me tomorrow night! I don't have to work this time! Got the night off!" She lifted both of her arms in the air in a "Waddaya say?" kind of motion.

Milty whined. "I don't know."

"Please?" Diane asked. Her arms were still outstretched. On display. She was putting herself completely out there and Milty was quite literally keeping her hanging.

Milty moaned. "How 'bout I think on it? Get back to you tomorrow?"

Diane dropped her arms and scowled into the dark. She knew he couldn't see her shadowed face at that distance. Without offering another word or acknowledgment that she'd heard his lame, yet expected equivocation, she turned on her heels and stormed back to the concession stand.

Chapter Four

Milty Burkitts

PLAY ▷

The Fry Fry

"The best damn fries on the planet."

That's what the sign said. Above the counter. Next to a cartoon of an anthropomorphic globe with neon pink sunglasses. At The Fry Fry. Milty scrunched up his face and focused on his bacon avocado burger. It dripped grease over his wrist and onto the still-steaming pile of potato slivers. They were good, of course, but *the best*? *On the planet*?

"Now, that's a bridge too far," he said to no one, "but they are just fine for my—"

"Milty?"

His burger hung suspended in front of his open mouth. He'd skipped breakfast—

I always skip breakfast.

—and his stomach rumbled wistfully at the piece of juicy meat just inches away from being digested. A voice spoke from somewhere behind him. He recognized it immediately because *of course* he did. It was the most beautiful sound he'd ever heard—sweet, sweet intonations he hadn't encountered much at all over the previous four years—and its owner was one he'd crushed on for the better part of his life. So perfect and yet so incredibly out of his league.

Out of my league, my world, my galaxy. All of the above.

He gulped, placed his burger down, closed his mouth, and forced himself to turn around.

"Velma? Hey. Wow, what a—um, surprise. Home at last, huh? The weary traveler returns."

She smiled at his awkwardness. It never had appeared to bother her, or at least—Milty thought—she was a kind enough person to pretend she didn't notice it. She sat down across from him at one of the other tall barstools at his table. Her blonde hair was done up in a messy bun and she was wearing a maroon, oversized, UMASS sweatshirt.

"Yeah," she said, taking a sip of her shake. "Just for a couple of days, though. Like to be home for homecoming, ya know? It's the easiest time to catch up with everyone from high school—" she stopped herself, remembering Milty hadn't ever left. She blushed a little and shifted uncomfortably on her stool, trying to find a way out of the ickiness she'd stepped in. "Mostly, though, I thought it'd be a good time to bring Rex home to finally meet everyone. My boyfriend. I'm not sure if you heard—" She put her drink down. "There he is."

Milty half-assed a look over his shoulder. A blonde-dreaded, blonde-bearded, blonde chest-haired borderline model floated over carrying a tray of food. He was wearing a skin-tight, tie-dye tank top, even though it was October, and a bright blue headband with the phrase "Be Wise" printed on it. The band pulled his dreads up into a bun and exposed a veiny temple that, impossibly, seemed to pulse in rhythm with his footsteps. Milty stifled a groan by stuffing his burger back into his face.

You have got to be kidding me.

The tanned college yogi—or whatever he was—settled into the last remaining chair at the table and pushed the food toward Velma. "Order's up, Sunshine."

She kissed him. "Rex, this is my old friend Milty."

Rex brought a forkful of salad—it looked to be lettuce and, not much else—to his mouth. He chewed carefully, brow furrowed as if he was taking his time to formulate a response, and then locked eyes with him. "Milty—I—hmm. Not sure I've heard your name before. Sorry, Bud. Were you and Velma, uh—friends? Or something?"

Milty nodded and angrily continued to eat. Through a mouthful of burger, he said, "Uh huh."

Velma made a valiant attempt to bridge the gap. She tapped the table. "Milty used to sit behind me in AP Chemistry. If I ever started to nod off in class, he would kick the back of my chair. Frickin' lifesaver this guy. I probably wouldn't have graduated if not for him."

Rex pretended to show interest, though his gaze was on his pile of greens. "Wow, that's—impressive, Bro. You're a hero, for sure."

This wasn't how Milty had envisioned his reunion with Velma going. Ideally, she would have seen him from afar, effortlessly cresting a wave. In his dreams, he'd jog up onto the beach, shake the salt water out of his frizzy hair, and distractedly half-wave to her as if he weren't completely preoccupied by her sudden appearance.

This is...not the same.

"No," he said, unsure of how to even respond to Rex's sarcasm. "No, not at all. It wasn't a big deal. It was just—I mean anyone would've done the same thing."

So smooth.

Rex shrugged and barely managed a head bob, clearly not even fully listening.

Velma took another sip of her smoothie, looking back and forth between the two. "So. Milty, you're coming to the bonfire tonight, right? I want Rex to meet as many of you as possible."

"*You?*" Milty seethed. *What "You" are you talking about, Velma? I'm not sure I was ever part of a "You".*

"I—" he started before correcting himself. "No, no. No, I don't think so. I'm not really feeling—"

Velma stuck out her bottom lip. "Aw, why not? Come on, you *have* to come."

Milty rocked his head back and forth, pretending to consider this thing that he was most definitely *not* considering. "You know, I just—well, I'm working a lot, ya know? I'm like *super* swamped at work. Late, late nights and all. Gotta stay on my game."

Rex blinked, his bloodshot eyes only half-open. "What do you... *do*?"

Milty choked a little on a piece of burger bun. "Uh, *do*? You mean—?"

Rex swallowed. "Yes, *do*. What do you *do*? For *work*?" He spoke with a side of his upper lip raised as if he was disgusted to even have to ask the question.

You walked right into this.

Milty opened his mouth but, before he could respond in kind, Velma interjected. "He works at Bay Video. Right over there," she pointed vaguely in the direction of the store. "Just behind the dune. It's always hoppin' late at night, right Milty?" She'd added that last part, presumably in a benevolent attempt to save him from any further embarrassment.

He nodded. "Yep. Exactly. So... *hoppin'*."

There was a long pause during which everyone chewed or sipped but no one spoke. Velma tried to pick up the slack again, after a moment. "So, what do you think? You gonna join us or not?" He shrugged and she kept going. "Come on, Milty! Come to the bonfire. It'll be fun and you'll get to know Rex a bit more. Please, for old times' sake?"

What old times?

Milty looked at Velma, then looked at Rex. He took another bite of his burger and swallowed it along with the cheeky retort he'd been about to throw back at the couple. "Oh, I—I dunno. As fun as all that sounds—" Velma stuck out her bottom lip again and he decided to soften the blow a bit. "Maybe. Ok? *Maybe*. We'll see how my shift goes."

That's the best I can offer, Velma. A "maybe". Only slightly more hopeful than the "How 'bout I think on it?" offered to Diane. A "maybe" is all I got. And, for anyone else, I probably wouldn't even go that far.

Velma seemed to accept his ambiguity and that she'd pushed him as far as she was going to be able. "Okay, well—I hope we see you there, Milty." She stood up and Rex followed her without saying goodbye. Velma waved and the two walked toward the parking lot.

Milty sighed and let his forehead thwack against the table.

Well, shit. You total coward. That was terrible.

He sat up and a pickle that'd managed to adhere itself to his temple fell back to earth. He shoved a couple of fries in his mouth and exhaled deeply.

"Best damn fries on the planet...my ass."
And then, he finished the rest.

CHAPTER FIVE

DIANE SHAW

PLAY ▷

Bay Video

DIANE LEANED ON THE counter and kept her eyes fixed on the TV screen that hung suspended over Milty's head. An actor in cartoonish vampire makeup hissed at a glowing green stone and she couldn't hold in a giggle, even though the scene was intended to scare audiences. Milty, who was busy pouring liquid butter over a brand-new batch of popcorn, raised an eyebrow but didn't look up from his task.

"What?" he said.

Diane snorted. "It's just *so* bad." She waited for a response from him and, when she didn't get one, continued. "Don't get me wrong, I love this movie. But it's one of those 'so bad it's good' things, right? It's like if you took *The Goonies* and mashed it together with all the Universal horror monsters. It's awesome—but, I mean, *come on*. I sorta feel like they didn't even try with this makeup design."

The movie was *The Monster Squad*. It seemed to always be playing at Bay Video, probably because no one ever rented it, and Diane was happy to stand and watch it whenever she dropped in. On top of that, Milty didn't seem to mind her public proselytizing on the film's virtues and faults. Or, at least, *she thought* he didn't mind. Milty always came across to her like a poker player, never showing any of his cards. So, she supposed, she could never truly be certain what he thought of her. Regardless, that she knew the movie so well and could talk about it for such long stretches gave Diane a perfect excuse to spend time with him.

Oh, Milty. You stupid, beautiful, creature.

He stunned her then by bringing up that evening's bonfire. "You—uh—you still planning on going tonight?"

Diane licked her lips. They were chapped. Could Milty tell? She wasn't sure. She hoped not.

"I—well, I don't really want to go *alone* again. The last few times, I ended up a third wheel to like five other couples and when it got late and a few too many beers had been had—well, let's just say that I ended up walking home alone each of those nights so I didn't have to *bare* witness to their skinny-dipping sessions."

Milty nodded but didn't even register a half-smile at her obvious pun. She couldn't tell if he was just distracted or genuinely didn't think she was funny. "Yeah, yeah, I get not wanting to be there for that."

Diane leaned over the counter just as a man transformed into a werewolf on the TV screen. "So, you gonna come?"

Milty shook his head and slammed the glass door on the popcorn machine closed. "No. No, I'm not and—"

"Oh, *come on,* Milty."

"—and before you say anything—"

"Why not?"

"—before you say anything—"

"It's because Velma's back and her hot new boyfriend is with her and you are too much of a chickenshit to go because he's all muscly and you still are crushing way hard on her."

A little harsh, Diane, but it had to be said.

Milty swallowed and lifted his eyes to meet hers. He blinked and then walked around the counter, heading toward the back of the shop. Diane followed him. She could see that his face was beet red and kept her distance as he stopped in front of a row of romantic comedies, needlessly straightening a few tapes that'd fallen over. On a copy of *Pretty in Pink*, Molly Ringwald stared blankly past him, directly at Diane—almost urging her to say something.

"I'm sorry," she said. "I shouldn't have—"

"No, no," he interrupted. "It's fine. You're not exactly wrong. I guess I just didn't realize that you knew—"

She sighed. "Of course, I know. I mean, *everyone* does, I think, at this point. You've been crushin' on Velma since we were in elementary school. It's...*obvious*, sir."

He turned to face her. "Well, damn."

"And," she continued, "I heard she was going to be there. Velma. I mean, I ran into her and her boyfriend before I came to the shop today. Guess I just assumed you did too."

Milty raised his eyebrows and was about to say something when the bell over the main entrance chimed. Surge walked in carrying a stack of movies from the rental return box outside. He didn't immediately see the two of them at the back of the store and called out to his employee.

"Milty? Hello? You here, Son?"

Milty stood on his tiptoes and peered over the top of a row of movies. "In the back, Surge."

Diane heard Surge curse under his breath. "Well, hurry on and get your ass up here. I've got a boatload of movies needing to be scanned in and reshelved. Not gonna do it themselves."

Milty gave Diane a look that said, "conversation's over" and then walked back to the counter. "I'm on it, Surge."

Diane followed him to the front. "It was my fault. I was talking his ear off again. I take full responsibility."

The store owner laughed and offered a playful reprimand. "Dammit, Shaw. I told you I cannot afford another employee right now. You spend so much time here I feel like you expect I'm gonna start paying you."

Diane leaned on the counter. The movie was still playing and a teenager in a black leather jacket was pointing a crossbow at some approaching vampires. She smirked. "Nossir. I'm just hanging out." She punched Milty in the shoulder. "What am I to do? Your staff is just so darn cute, I can't stay away."

Wow, so we're...we're comin' in hot today.

Milty groaned and Surge responded with a hearty guffaw, hoarse from years of cigar smoking. "Well, you know you are always welcome. Though, I wish you would rent something. This *is* a goddamn business, you know?"

Diane smiled but didn't commit to paying for anything just then. "Yeah, yeah." She moved closer to Milty again. "Well, guess I'm gonna head out, Sir. So, you're a 'no' for tonight then? Solidly?"

Milty nodded.

Diane pursed her lips and flicked at the brim of her Drive-In cap in annoyance. "Cool, well—" she started moving toward the door. "I hope you have a good—"

Surge materialized again from wherever he'd disappeared to. He was sweating and breathing heavily, as if he'd just run up a flight of stairs, but Diane was pretty certain he'd done nothing more than a lap to the rear of the store and back. "I hear you talkin' about that bonfire? He's going tonight, right? You make sure this boy—"

Diane lifted her eyebrows and shrugged. "I tried."

Milty pretended to be fiddling with the popcorn machine again until Surge grabbed his shoulders and spun him around to face Diane. "Son, this pretty lady has asked you nicely to join her at that damn bonfire tonight and for godssakes you are gonna join her at that bonfire tonight if it kills me."

"Surge—"

"No, don't you do that. Don't you *Surge* me. You're going."

"I—"

"It's settled. And, to make sure you go and that you have absolutely zero excuses, I'm even gonna let you outta work early tonight so you can have a proper shower and shit." He put his hands up. "I'll still pay ya for the hour, so long as you promise to go."

Milty looked at his feet for a moment before meeting Surge's squinty gaze and finally letting his scowl come to rest on Diane. "Fine. *Fine.* I'll... I'll go."

Surge smiled. Diane smiled.

"Happy now?" Milty asked.

Diane nodded. She could feel her face warming and tried to stifle the Jack-o-lantern smirk she knew was blossoming. "Oh, yes. Very."

Surge slapped Milty on the back and then pointed at Diane. "You make sure he doesn't try to sneak home too early tonight, ya hear?"

Diane mock saluted him. "Aye aye, Captain." She walked to the front door and then pointed at Milty. "Meet ya there, then?"

He gave a thumbs up but looked visibly annoyed. A large vein pulsed on his temple.

"Don't chicken out on me now."

He's totally going to.

Milty waved her off. "I won't. But, I gotta get back to work. I'm leaving early tonight now, I guess."

Diane smiled at him and then let her lungs fill with the sweet, stale air of the rental shop. As the door swung shut behind her, another familiar smell—a wave of buttered popcorn— trailed after. It tickled her flared nostrils and she nearly skipped out into the late afternoon sun.

CHAPTER SIX

MILTY BURKITTS

PLAY ▷

The Bonfire

WIND FROM EARLIER IN the day had left the wooden path between the dunes sand-covered, and Milty's feet—supported only by flimsy, foam-covered flip-flops—slipped multiple times as he approached the beach. Being October, the sun was already setting—even though it wasn't long past dinnertime. At Surge's urging, Milty had gone home early, had a quick bite to eat, and showered. He'd squandered a few minutes preposterously deliberating over which ratty Cape Cod hooded-sweatshirt to wear (they all were variations of the same, collar-torn, salt and sun-bleached look) and eventually settled on a cranberry-colored one that had a big blue shark-fin on it.

As he approached the end of the path, a slight breeze kicked up and the grass on the dunes crackled and tittered at him. A few stray, dry, yellowish appendages tickled his bare legs—Milty wore shorts year round—as he walked past. Sparks from a fire already lit and some raised voices told him the party had started without him—

And why wouldn't it?

—and a dense ocean fog rolled in heavily from off the bay. He'd reached the very end of the path, and was about to step out onto the hours-cold sand, when he noticed a shadow standing—waiting—right at the base of the dune. He stopped.

"Hello?"

The form didn't move or respond to the sound of his voice. He gulped and took a few steps forward.

"Hello? Who's—?"

Diane spun around, grinning.

"*Finally*," she hissed, a smile giving away her intense amusement. "What took you so long?"

"Had to eat. Had to shower. Had to—"

She stopped him with a squeeze of his elbow. He couldn't remember her ever making physical contact with him, beyond the occasional playful punch, and he didn't hate it.

"I'm kidding. I'm kidding," she said. "Honestly, I'm just shocked you actually showed up for once."

"Yeah, me too. Haven't made it to one of these since our high school days. And even then it was...*rare*."

They each kicked their flip-flops off and left them in the mountain of footwear piled at the end of the walkway.

Diane pulled him toward the fire. Her hair was tied up in a messy-bun and she was wearing a white lifeguard sweatshirt. The lettering on it was red. "Well, it's about damn time."

Milty thought, as they approached the group and a few curious faces swiveled in their direction, that he'd heard her whisper to herself, "I'm just really glad you're here," but he didn't have time to respond before they were both warmly greeted.

It wasn't a huge group by any means, which—in Milty's eyes—wasn't a bad thing at all. A couple of hugs were exchanged, a back slap, a fist bump, and then Milty found an open spot on a piece of drift wood that'd been dragged over. Diane squeezed herself in beside him.

Say something. Don't be weird. They're all staring at you.

"Hey everyone," he said to the five others who also sat on pieces of wood encircling the fire. The conflagration was already fairly large and probably would've been easy to spot from a mile or so away—at least—considering how little a curve this stretch of beach had.

"Surprised you guys made it," Velma said, "but I'm really happy to see you both." She was sitting on a log next to Rex and her fingers were intertwined with his. She made an obvious show of looking back and forth between Milty and Diane, squinting her eyes as if she were trying to solve some sort of puzzle. "So, are you two like...*you know?*"

For a minute, Milty didn't catch what she was suggesting, and then—when he saw Diane grinning like a mad fool—it dawned on him. "Oh, ah—wow. No, *no*. Oh gosh, no."

He felt Diane slide a little further away from him.

Velma laughed. "Oh, sorry. I just thought—well—you both arrived together and are sitting together and—"

Milty looked to Diane who'd pulled her hood over her head. "I mean, it's not that Diane isn't—uh, I guess what I'm trying to say is—ah, *shit*. I mean, it's just not like *that* with the two of us but—"

Diane stopped him again with a grab of his elbow, albeit with a less-gentle touch this go around. "It's ok, Milty. You can stop." She looked up at Velma. "We're just friends, Vel."

He saw Velma mouth an "I'm sorry," to Diane, who waved it off.

Well, that was a fantastic freaking start to the evening. Bravo. Well done you asshat.

He couldn't bring himself to turn and face Diane but could feel her staring daggers into the side of his head. Instead of offering an apology, he let his focus flick to all the others who'd gathered that evening, offering each a polite nod as his eyes met theirs.

Seated on the opposite side of Velma and Rex was Kyle Crowell. He sported a freshly cut, freshly gelled mohawk down the middle of his head. Milty and Kyle had gotten along fairly well as kids but, as they'd grown older—and Kyle'd barely evolved or matured in any significant way—the two had only drifted further and further apart.

Not that you're such great shakes, Milty thought. *Remember, he's not the only one still living in his parent's basement.*

Like Milty, Kyle hadn't left for college and was still working around town. Even worse, he drove his mom's minivan.

Is that worse, though? At least he has a ride.

Milty lifted a hand and waved. In response, Kyle belched loudly and tossed a beer can into the fire. The person next to him—Dale Fenton, another long-time local fixture—pointed at it.

"Hey, Dumbass. You do know aluminum doesn't burn, right?"

Kyle, Dale's best-friend, belched again and then put up both middle fingers. "Double freedom rockets, ba-by!"

Dale put his hand on his chest, taking mock-offense. "Hey, now. Not in front of the lady!" The "lady", of course, was Beatrix Starling—Dale's girlfriend since, well— *forever.*

"Hi, Milty. Hi Diane." Beatrix offered warmly. "Haven't seen either of you in a while. It's been a minute."

Milty finally looked at Diane and she took her hood off. She was smiling, perhaps a sign that she'd already moved beyond his earlier transgression. "Hey, B," she said. "I really like your hair tonight. It's... *big.*"

Beatrix fluffed at it. "Oh, thank you, I—"

"Used half a can of hairspray. Easily," Dale cut her off.

Beatrix swatted at him. "Well, it takes a lot to keep this demon under control."

Milty couldn't tell if she was referring to her hair, herself, or Dale. All were possibilities.

Something popped in the fire and a huge plume of spark danced into the sky. Orion and his belt were clearly visible overhead, and the constellation appeared to be commanding the flames higher and higher.

"Beer? Milty? Diane?" It was Rex. He had a can in each hand and wagged them in their direction. Diane grabbed hers without hesitating, offering a quick "Thanks" and Milty, wanting to play along, eventually did the same.

"Thank you," Milty said. "How long you guys home for, by the way? I mean—here, in Eastham."

"Just the weekend," Velma said, with a touch of sadness in her voice. "Wish it could be longer, but gotta be back for class on Monday morning."

Diane slurped her beer and Milty followed suit. "Ah, that's too bad," he said and then, in an attempt to avoid appearing as if he was only talking to Velma, added to Rex, "So, you ever been down the Cape before?"

Rex took a long glug. "Nah, Bro. First visit." He locked eyes with Milty. "And I plan on making it a good one."

Milty felt uncomfortable with how long the other held his gaze and he looked away. "Oh? What, uh—you got any specific plans while you're here? Not that there's much going on in October around this way."

Velma turned to Rex, shook her head, and then faced Milty. He didn't know what to make of the interaction but hadn't much time to ponder what it could've meant before she spoke.

"Oh, well—he's got all these goofy ideas...but we're *not* going to bore all of you with any of that tonight. We're here to party and then—"

Likely picking up on her hesitation, Beatrix chimed in. "It's no bore. Tell us. What's he got cookin'?"

Velma looked a little uncomfortable. Milty looked from Beatrix, to her, to Rex. "It's nothing, really," she insisted. "I'd rather we not—"

Rex rolled his eyes. "Why can't I tell them?" he grumbled.

Velma leaned closer to him. "Just leave it alone, ok?"

"But, *why*? Why do you care so much?"

"We talked about this, remember? I explained it to you." She forced a smile. "More than once."

Kyle belched again. "Screw it, we're just sitting around shooting the shit. What's the big effing secret?"

"Yeah, let the guy tell us," Dale added. "Why you acting so weird, Vel?"

Velma sighed and waved at Rex who seemed to take that as approval to speak.

He stood then as if he were making an announcement. The fire lit him, orange illuminating his sinewy frame from head to foot. Even with the crispness of the fall evening, he'd somehow found reason to wear a sweatshirt that hung low enough to expose most of his chest. *Give me a break.*

"Well," Rex Templeton said, pointing his beer can dramatically toward the sea. "There are stories about this place, this bay. Stories that stretch to ears and minds far beyond the Cape, over your Bourne and Sagamore bridges. Beyond the Berkshire Mountains. Stories that—for people like me, people who've never been here before—need to be investigated."

Velma sagged a bit on the log.

Everyone was quiet, inexplicably enraptured by the man's speech. And it wasn't just *what* he said. There was also a certain power in his voice—that of a trained orator accustomed to audiences hanging on his every word. He waited, obviously wanting one of them to ask for more.

Milty scoffed. *Yeah, well. I'm not giving you what you want. Someone else is going to have to—*

"What needs to be investigated?" Dale asked. "What stories?"

Rex smiled and, as he basked in the vermilion light, appeared on the edge of a diabolical fit. He cackled and another pop sounded, on cue, in the fire. "What can you all tell me about—"

"Rex, don't," Velma pleaded.

"—*the Buoygeist?*"

Nobody gasped but everyone immediately tensed. Dale had a beer at his lips and he carefully lowered it. Beatrix sat up straighter. Kyle looked behind himself into the night. And Diane reached over and squeezed Milty's elbow again, perhaps absentmindedly. Perhaps not.

So, this is where he's going with this? For chrissakes. How regrettably predictable. Classic tourist bullshit of the highest degree.

"Rex," Velma stood up. "I told you about this. You *promised*."

He cracked his neck. "I know, I *know* you did. I *know* I promised. But, I mean—*man*—it's *the Buoygeist*. And I'm here. I'm here where the story *lives*. Finally. How can I not, at least—ya know—*ask*?"

Nobody said anything for a few beats until Milty stood up. As he spoke, he heard his own voice but was shocked by the conviction and confidence that poured out of him. Before he had even a moment to reconsider whether or not he even wanted to give air to what he knew the rest of the group would've preferred just went by the wayside, he launched into an angry admonishment of Velma's boyfriend.

"I don't want to speak for anyone else, but—you're new—you don't understand how things work around here. I'll cut you a break if you just leave it be. There've probably been many over the years like you, tourists, people just passing through who don't get it. To be fair, how could they? But we—" he looked around at the others gathered there on that evening. "We just don't ever talk about *that*. Like—*ever*."

Rex let his arms remain suspended in the air as he looked from face to face. "No one? Not ever?"

Velma whispered into his ear. "No. But, I already told you that. And now you're embarrassing me."

Rex raised his voice. "I'm *embarrassing* you? How? How am I embarrassing you?"

Milty didn't like how Rex was speaking to her. He didn't move, Diane was still holding on to him even from her seated position, but he did raise his voice to match the other's. "Why don't you just leave it alone, Rex?"

Rex's eyes went wide and he swung his head to meet Milty's challenge. It was evident that people rarely spoke to him in such a manner and that any attempts to put him in his place were likely few and far between. His pupils reflected the fire and tiny flames burned from his orbital sockets devilishly. "Why Milty? Tell me. Why should I? What—you aren't afraid of a little ghost story, are you?"

Milty didn't answer but Diane spoke up in his defense. "So, what if he is? What do you even know about this? He told you that everyone around here prefers not to talk about it. I'm sure Velma told you the very same thing. Some legends are best forgotten. You asked us what we thought about this and Milty answered. You know what we think about it. Now, don't be an asshole and push this further. It's incredibly clear that you have no idea what you're even asking."

Yes, Diane. Well, said.

Rex, exasperated, punched at the air and kicked a flaming log. More sparks shot up and a cloud of smoke hit Milty square in the face. He coughed, covering his mouth and nose.

"Jesus, Rex," Velma said and grabbed at his sleeve. "You're drunk. Let's just go home and—"

He ignored her, pulling his arm away. "But, see," he squinted as if looking for a name tag. "Diane, is it? You're right, you know. I *don't* know about this, which is *why* I'm asking. I've heard things, interesting things, and so—I *ask*. Does no one want to tell me about this Buoygeist fella?" When no one answered, he tried again. "And why not? Don't tell me you actually *believe* any of this shit. You don't, right?"

Finally, Milty'd had enough and took a step closer to him. "Not that I feel the need to explain things to you, but... efforting to move this conversation along—if it matters—I'm not sure *believe* is the right word. Not exactly." He looked to Diane and then to Velma for encouragement and, when they both nodded in his direction, he continued. "It's kind of like... just something people around here learn to live with. The stories, I mean. And, I'm not sure if anyone believes them but we—I dunno—*respect* them. I guess." He looked to the others who'd grown up in the area, hoping for a bit of support. "Am I explaining this right, guys?"

A few others nodded in agreement.

"Good enough," Dale said in support.

They all remained motionless, waiting for someone to break the silence. A few waves crashed close by. It was nearing high tide and the ocean was alerting them of its imminent approach.

"Anyway," Milty tried to wrap it up. "I think, on that note, it's probably time for me to call it a night—"

Rex stepped closer to him, so close that Milty thought he was going to give him a hug.

"Hold up. So, where is this buoy anyway? Is it far from here?"

"Rex," Velma said, pleading with him. "Time to go."

"I—I don't know if it's a good idea—"

"Rex—"

"What're—are you afraid to tell me or something, Milty?"

Milty pursed his lips. Rex was challenging him in front of everyone else. In front of Velma. In front of Diane. He didn't want to tell him but also didn't want to appear—what was Diane's word from earlier that day—*chickenshit*?

"Well?" Rex said, his nose almost touching Milty's.

Milty swallowed hard and then spoke. "The marina."

Rex nodded. Perhaps he'd already known. "The marina. About how far? Close by? I think I want to see this thing."

Diane stood up then. "Okay. Milty, come on. That's enough. I wanna go home. *Now.*"

Milty didn't turn but kept his eyes locked on to Rex's. He was trying not to blink. Velma was over Rex's shoulder, attempting to pull him in the other direction.

"Rex, I'm tired. Please. This isn't funny."

"Milty, will you walk me home?" Diane petitioned again. "I don't like this. We shouldn't do this."

Somehow, Rex's eyes got even wider. "Well?"

Milty tucked some of his massive curls more tightly under his foam Eastham trucker hat. A bead of sweat trickled down his temple, despite the chilly October air. His thin frame stood tall, his chest nearly touching Rex's.

"Fine," he said not believing the words coming out of his mouth. *"Let's fucking go."*

Chapter Seven

Milty Burkitts

PLAY ▷

The Marina

"That's it?"

The seven stood out at the end of the dock. Moored boats bobbed innocently to the left and right, and all eyes fixated on a dark shape that rose and fell with each wave. Though it couldn't have hovered more than a few hundred yards from where they huddled—just beyond the main thoroughfare that most vessels passed through and just before the first weedy vestiges of the marsh began breaching the surface—the light from the Harbormaster's office didn't reach that far out into the water nor did the minimal lighting from the parking lot. The shape was barely visible. An inky, blurry blob. Its lack of definition only proved to further exacerbate their angst and the disquiet blanketing their already shivering souls.

When no one answered, Rex repeated himself as if he hadn't already spoken. "That's it? I was expecting..."

"What *were* you expecting?" Milty snapped. "It's a buoy. An old rusty buoy. Sorry to disappoint, but it is what it is. Can we go now?"

The dock creaked underneath them. Rex was hypnotized by the enigmatic shadow and ignored Milty's question. Deep in thought, he squatted down, closer to the water, and clasped his well-manicured hands. Though Rex made every attempt to appear the earthy-crunchy, knee-deep-in-nature type, it was clear his hands had never seen a day's worth of real labor. He'd lived an entitled life—or so Milty supposed with almost nothing else to go on—and everything else about him was a massive put-on. "Anyone got a flashlight?" Even in the dark, the dreadlocked trust-fund kid's grin was unnerving. Not unlike the Cheshire Cat's hovering, toothy sneer.

"No, none of us have a flashlight, Rex." He pointed out in the direction of the buoy. "Ok, so you've seen it. There it is. Happy now? Let's get going and—"

"Woah, woah, woah," the man in the dreads stopped him, holding out his perfectly moisturized hands. "We've come this far. Let's go take a closer look, huh?"

Most of the group started moving back toward the parking lot. All except Rex Templeton and Milty Burkitts.

"Rex, it's dark. Even if we had a boat—it's just not safe. The Harbormaster isn't here, it's pitch-black and—"

Rex called to Velma just as she reached the sand-covered edge of the pavement. "Is this the marina your dad's boat is docked at?"

Velma turned and stared blankly back at him, her arms wrapped around themselves. She was shivering, but Milty couldn't tell if it was because of the cold or because she was scared. "No, Rex. I mean—*yes*, this is where his boat is—but, *no*, we're not taking it out there. People don't just—*go out there*. People don't *take a closer look*."

Rex laughed. "Why not? What could possibly happen?"

No one answered.

Milty was the only one still standing out at the end of the dock. Rex playfully slapped him in the stomach. "You actually believe this shit?"

I'm just tired. Tired of this night and tired of trying to explain it to you.

"I dunno, Rex. It's getting late. You're starting to upset everyone." He pointed to the crowd waiting for them at the opposite end of the dock. "Why don't we—?"

"No. Uh, uh," he interrupted. "We've come this far, haven't we? Hey, Vel, which is your dad's boat? I promise I just wanna take a quick peek, see what all the fuss is about, and then we can get outta here. Please? *Please*? I'm begging."

"Rex—"

"Please, Baby. Who knows when we'll be back here?"

Velma rubbed her arms.

"I don't know. My dad will kill me."

Rex clasped his hands together, pleading to her. "We won't tell him." He mimed zipping up his lips. "He'll never know. He'll never find out. Cross my heart and hope to—"

"Don't say it. Just don't—" Velma sighed. The wind picked up a bit and her blonde hair whipped about, her locks catching a bit of the Harbormaster's light. "I guess—I guess so."

Rex thumped himself on the chest and howled at the moon. "This is going to rock."

"But, only for a few minutes. In and out."

Milty watched as the man ran back down the dock and lifted Velma high into the air. They locked lips for an interminable amount of time before he placed her gently onto the ground again. He turned to Milty, who was now standing by himself in the shadows right at the water's edge.

"You comin', Broseph?"

Begrudgingly, he nodded and followed after them. Though the rest were all moving with Velma toward her father's docked boat, Diane waited for him. Her eyes were wide. Scared.

"Can we just go? They don't need us, right?"

He shook his head.

"But this is so stupid, Milty. Seriously. We've all heard the stories. I'm legitimately scared right now."

He walked past her and, when he spoke, wasn't sure if what he said in response was aloud or in his head.

"Yeah. Me too, Diane. Me too."

CHAPTER EIGHT

VELMA GREEN

PLAY ▷

The Boat

EVERYONE PILED IN. MILTY helped by untying the mooring and, at Velma's signal, pushed them away from the dock. The engine was running and she let the boat drift astern for a bit before turning the wheel so they all faced forward in the direction she knew the buoy to be in.

As a kid, her dad—as did all local dads whose brains had been sufficiently brined in the waters of Cape Cod Bay—warned her to never get too close to the floating piece of rusted metal out on the far side of the inlet. He'd always said it was because of the shallow bed at that particular point in the creek, but she knew he had additional—altogether more dubious—reasoning. Not that he'd ever fully elaborated on his thinking, nor had he ever really needed to. It was a superstition shared widely and she couldn't remember anyone ever questioning it. She'd crossed her heart as a little girl and told him she'd never venture to that side of the waterway.

Yet, here I am. In the middle of the night. Finally breaking my promise. And, for what?

She gulped.

Sorry, Dad. Home for just a couple of days. Didn't figure things would take me here.

She glanced at Rex who lay, stretched out, at the bow of the boat—another thing her dad had requested she and her friends never do—and wondered why he looked so eager, so *hungry*. Why did he suddenly feel like such a stranger? Velma thought she'd had a solid read on him. Rex Templeton. Captain of the Ultimate Frisbee Team and drum circle extraordinaire. Laid-back, unapologetic about his perpetually bare feet, and loving the smell of his own patchouli. How could she *not* know him? Dating a guy for half of a college year was certainly no easy feat, after all. It required, she'd convinced herself, a great deal of commitment, and—as such—she'd dedicated a large chunk of her time just *being* with him. He'd seemed, more than any other guy she'd dated, to really want to get to know her and—perhaps more than anything—seemed truly interested in meeting her friends, her family, and visiting the place she'd grown up in.

Didn't think for a second our first night in town would look like this.

The others were all huddled together in the stern. Dale had his arms wrapped around B, Kyle sat on the other side of her, and Diane shivered quietly next to Milty.

Velma almost laughed. *Milty, Buddy. You're missing a prime opportunity here.*

She knew where Milty's real feelings resided. She always had, in fact, and it hadn't ever bothered her. He was never pushy and, if anything, she found his polite—albeit long-lasting—crush on her to be incredibly sweet. He wasn't her type *at all* but she did think he was the real deal. An honest-to-God *good* human. And that was far more than she could say for a lot of people.

When she turned back to the bow, Rex was staring at her.

"You ready for this, Sunshine?" It was dark, but she could still see the crazed look in his eyes.

What is up with you?

She cut the engine and let the boat drift a bit. They were only a few yards away.

"Whatever, Rex. Can we just get this over with?"

He rolled his eyes at her. "Aw, come on. This is fun. *Relax*. Live a little."

Velma trembled as she felt the cold breath of the Atlantic whisper a warning into her ear. Everyone was silent in the back. It was obvious that all but Rex were uncomfortable and probably sharing in the trepidation she was currently feeling. "Grab it as we go by," she said to him.

He did and she let the gunwale of the boat side up to the buoy. There was a loud screeching as they dragged against it.

Rex rubbed his hands together.

"Okay, gang." He grinned as the moonlight glinted off of his perfect, too-white teeth. "Now what?"

CHAPTER NINE

MILTY BURKITTS

PLAY ▶

The Buoy

"I THINK WE'VE TAKEN this far enough."

Milty was still seated next to Diane. Velma remained at the wheel and Rex was leaning over trying to get a closer look at the buoy.

"Oh, *stop*. We're already here. The least we could do is take a quick kick at the can. Right?" He rocked the thing back and forth a few times, examining it reverently as one might do with a dusty, priceless, relic found on an archeological dig. "So, what's the trick? I mean, what am I supposed to do?" he laughed. "Is there like an ancient phrase I need to repeat three times? Do I need to bleed on it or...*something*?"

No one answered and Rex's expression quickly went slack.

"Oh, for chrissakes, don't play dumb. I *know* you guys know. It's why you all look like you're gonna piss your pants right now."

Milty stood up. Diane grabbed his arm, but he gently pulled away from her. "Look, Rex. You've had your fun. Not only did we bring you to the marina, but you convinced Velma to drag her dad's boat out so you could get a closer look. Now you've seen it. But we've had enough. We're all tired and, in case you hadn't noticed, this is making us all a bit uncomfortable."

Rex was still holding on to the buoy. His dreads were hanging so low they almost skimmed the surface of the water. "Interesting. But, uh—then why'd you come? You came all the way out here, but—what—*now* you just wanna turn around?" He looked from Milty to Velma and back to Milty again. "Why'd you even get in the boat?"

Milty pursed his lips. He locked eyes with Velma. "What do you want me to say? Guess we didn't wanna leave Velma alone with—"

"With *me*?" Rex growled. "That what you were gonna say? With *me*? Hilarious this guy, huh, Sunshine?"

Velma reached out and touched his outstretched leg. "Rex. We all want to go back. Can you just let go of the buoy now?"

Or you could just stay out here by yourself. Either way.

Milty kept the thought inside.

"Sunshine. *Babe.* I will. I promise I will. Just—just tell me what happens next. Do that and—yes, then I'll let go."

This guy keeps on moving the goalposts.

Dale'd had enough and he shrugged out from underneath Beatrix. "Bro, if we tell you will you finally knock this shit off? It's late. We're all freaking exhausted."

Rex grinned. "I already said I promised, *Dale.*"

Dale groaned and then unleashed a torrent. "You don't gotta *do* anything. Or—not exactly. Shit, I can't believe I'm even telling you this." He closed his eyes and spat out the rest. "You just gotta, sort of, *want* it. To happen."

Rex shook his head. "Want what? What do you—?"

Finally, Diane rose. She pushed past Dale, then Milty, and stood beside Velma at the wheel. She lowered her voice as if whispering might make it easier to say what it was she wanted to tell him.

"Look, Rex. You're an idiot and you're messing around with something you shouldn't be. But, what Dale means is, you have it want it to...*open.*"

Rex was getting exasperated. He kept having to readjust his grip on the buoy. "I don't understand. Open? Open *what*? What is *it*?"

Diane bit her lip and pulled her hood up. "It's a gateway. Or—at least that's what the stories say. The stories we've grown up with. The stories that have been fed to us our entire lives."

Rex was finally getting what he wanted. "Ah *ha*. Now we're getting somewhere. Okay, so it's a gateway? A gateway to...*what*, exactly?"

Diane had the floor and, when no one else chimed in, she continued. In the moonlight, despite the topic of conversation, Milty found himself realizing how beautiful she was. The lunar glow reflected brilliantly off of her hair and either the cold or her agitation made the rosy color of her cheeks suddenly bloom.

"To Hell. It's a gateway to Hell. Or, that's what the legend says."

"To *Hell*?" Rex mocked her. "Give me a break, Diane."

She folded her arms, defensively. "Yeah. Or some kind of underworld prison. I dunno. There are many variations of the same story. It's an urban legend, so most of what we've all heard has sort of grown and evolved as the tale's been shared and retold over and over. What do you want me to say? You asked. And I'm probably not getting everything totally right, okay? We *don't* mess with it though. That I *do* know. It could be—no, it *definitely* is—total bullshit, but...why find out? Ya know?" She appeared to wait for another question from Rex, but he just stared at her. His mouth was open and Milty thought for an instant that the airhead might start drooling. After a few seconds, Diane spoke again. "It's supposed to unleash a demon or a spirit or *something* if—"

"If what?" Rex really wanted her to get to the *what*.

Diane looked around at all the other faces on the boat before warily responding. "Unclear. It's not like there's a ritual or...or anything like that. This isn't some dumb movie. We're not bustin' out our Ouija board. They say—they say someone's got to come out here and just *want* it. That's it. Like *really* want it."

The water sloshed under the boat as a rather large wave careened into them. Even in the darkness, Milty sensed Rex bracing himself so that he didn't topple over the side. The other passengers similarly grabbed for a steadier hold.

If any of us fall in and get caught in that current, there's not going to be help getting here anytime soon. We'd be up the creek without a—

"Want it?" Rex urged Diane to continue. Milty noticed a vein in his neck that looked like it was ready to burst.

Diane, don't indulge him.

She nodded and sighed deeply. It was evident she just wanted to get it all over it. "Yeah. They say that it won't come unless somewhere out here really *wants* its help. If that person exists and they look

down into those depths and...and *it* hears...then, then it'll return."
She swallowed. "*For one night.*"

Another wave crashed against the boat.

There. You have the info you need. Now, let's get the hell—

"It? You mean, the Buoygeist?" Rex let out a childlike giggle
that seemingly he hadn't been able to stifle. "Sounds like a bunch of
bullshit, Diane."

She flipped him off. "You dragged this outta us. We didn't want
to tell you. You're the one who *heard the stories* and wanted to see it,
remember?"

"Sure, I wanted to *see* it but—man, I also wanted to see Plymouth
Rock and I knew the Pilgrims didn't *literally* crash their boat into
that stupid piece of rubble. Ho-ly shit. Dudes, I didn't think in a
million years anyone actually took this seriously. You should see your
faces right now. Every single one of you needs to have your head
examined. *Wild.*"

Milty wanted to hit him but restrained himself.

Such a prick.

"Ok, enough's enough. I'm done." Velma gestured to everyone
in the stern to sit back down. "I'm starting the engine. You're either
gonna have to let go or end up in the water, Rex. Up to you."

For a second, it looked like he wouldn't release his grip but, just
as Velma put the vessel in reverse, he relented.

"Jesus, Vel. You really would have let me slip off into the water,
huh? Unbelievable. That's downright cold."

She tilted her head. "Yeah, well. You would have deserved it."

Slowly, the boat turned and began heading back toward the dock.
The creek was getting increasingly choppy and more than once the
craft came down hard after cresting a wave. Everyone was jostled
around, but Velma didn't slow the boat's progress.

I don't blame ya, Vel. We're all just so ready for this night to be over.

Rex was now sitting up straight in the bow, apparently needing
a change of position after an extended period spent lying on his
stomach. "Hey," he started again, eliciting more than a few groans
from the rest of the group. "Quick question. How're you all so
scared of this? Don't you think—after all this time, after all these

years—someone out there would have seen *something*? It'd be all over the news."

Diane was about to respond, but Milty decided to give her a break. "The truth is that the legend is framed perfectly to give storytellers an easy answer for all the doubters. Probably by design, of course, but—the Buoygeist—it's whole MO is—well, if you ever are actually successful in summoning it—if you *see* it—you—" he hesitated.

"You, what?" an exasperated Rex snarled.

"You *die*." Milty finished. "Hence no survivors. No one left to tell the tale."

Rex spat off the side of the boat. "Convenient."

Milty shrugged. "I told ya. Good storytelling. Kinda like all those people saying Bloody Mary into the mirror three times. Ya know? If they *see* her...well, you get the idea. And on the off chance anyone does survive the night, who'd believe 'em? Telling a story like this? You'd be locked up faster'n it'd take you to finish a bacon cheeseburger at The Fry Fry, I'd wager."

Rex smirked. "Also convenient. Feel like you've seen too many movies."

Milty looked at Diane who pursed her lips and nodded as if she agreed. "Yeah, maybe."

The skiff pulled up to the dock. Kyle jumped out on his own accord and started mooring the boat again. One by one, everyone—except for Velma and Rex—climbed back onto the wooden walkway.

"You coming, Vel?" Milty called to her.

She waved at him. "You guys go on ahead. Have to make sure this all looks in order. Don't want my dad to have any clue we were ever here."

As the rest of the group started, in one big clump, to walk back in the direction of the parking lot, Rex—still lost in his own thoughts—called up to them.

"Sweet dreams, suckers!"

Milty turned to say something but Diane gripped his elbow and he swallowed his sarcastic riposte.

Stay classy, Rex. Stay classy. I'll remember this moment when it comes for you first.

CHAPTER TEN

DIANE SHAW

PLAY ▷

103 Barnacle Cove Road

Why did you tell him all of that?

Diane was propped up on a pillow in bed, her hair wrapped high in a faded pink towel. She was wearing an extra-large Mickey Mouse t-shirt and black and yellow flannel pajama pants. Her hands were crossed over her chest and she twiddled her thumbs restlessly.

Now you've got to sit here, all alone in this house, and worry. If you'd just kept your dumb mouth shut—

The sound of a car door shutting somewhere outside made her jump. Likely Mrs. Evers across the street, getting home from a late shift at the hospital. Diane looked at the small black Radio Shack alarm clock on her side table. Its red lights blinked *10:15 pm*. Definitely Mrs. Evers. Right on schedule. She scrunched her eyes shut and massaged her forehead.

Probably wouldn't have mattered. Don't put this all on yourself, Diane. Rex would have dragged it out of someone else eventually anyway.

The timing couldn't have been worse, though. Her parents were away for the weekend, attending a friend's wedding in The Berkshires, and Diane had initially been stoked to have the place all to herself. Not that she was likely to be hosting a party of any sort, but she had planned to binge the first three *Jaws* movies and order a pizza. Maybe somewhere in the back of her mind—in her wildest, most

fantastical vision of how the evening could have unfolded—Diane
had even considered the possibility that Milty might walk her home
and join in on her movie marathon extravaganza.

*Extravaganza? You, serious Diane? In your pjs with a greasy
Hawaiian from Happy Joseph's House of Pizza? Yeah, I can't believe
Milty wouldn't have been down for that kind of party. And why the
hell is Happy Joseph so goddamned happy?*

She blew a bunch of air out through her lips in exasperation. The
night had not gone according to plan. Not even close. She'd finally
convinced Milty to join her at the bonfire and the guy had spent
more time puffing his chest out in front of Velma's boyfriend than he
had realizing Diane was also there, also a participant in the evening.
Not that Milty was unkind to her—in fact, he *never* was—but she
wished he'd stop obsessing so hard over something—*someone*—so
far beyond his reach. Everyone—quite literally *everyone* in the small,
sleepy, beachside town of Eastham—knew Velma didn't see him like
that.

*Sometimes I wish you'd just tell him, Vel. Put the guy out of his
misery AND give the rest of us a chance. A two birds with one stone
sort of deal.*

She pulled the towel off of her head and let her still-damp, red
hair fall onto her shoulders.

*Besides, I know of a certain someone who WOULD give him the
time of day. Like, all of the time. Of every day. What does a girl gotta
do to get this guy's attention?*

She took her neon green hairbrush from the drawer beside her
bed and began absentmindedly to pull it through the tangled mess.
It caught on a particularly bad snarl and she cursed under her breath.

"Ugh. So annoying. Why does my hair have to suck so bad?
Everyone else loves my curls but they've never lived with 'em. I just
wish I—"

Another sound from outside, but this time it was definitely *not*
Mrs. Evers getting home from the hospital. Diane had cracked her
window before settling into bed—despite the temperature out on
the water, it was still seasonally warm for an October evening on
the Cape—and probably wouldn't have heard the somewhat muted
noise otherwise.

What was that?

If there'd been intelligible words or language of any kind, she would have described the sound as a voice. But, after replaying the utterance in her head, she decided that wasn't exactly right. Whatever she'd heard was certainly a vocalization, hoarse and strained, one that'd carried some distance to her ears. It was faint, almost as if it'd been dispatched from far away, echoing up from the end of a long drain pipe or cave. But there were no words—at least nothing that she could decipher or distinguish.

Your imagination, Diane. That's all it is. You were already strung pretty high tonight. You're alone in the house. Anything you hear is gonna naturally set you off.

She pulled her hairbrush the rest of the way through a knot and then placed it on the bed. Gingerly, she stepped toward her window and pulled apart the lacey pink curtains—still hanging from when her grandmother had made them for Baby Diane some twenty years earlier.

Just take a quick look.

She breathed in deeply—

You can do it. There's nothing there.

—clenched her jaw—

If anything it's a coyote or something. Probably panting as it investigates some roadkill. Rabies has made its way over the bridge again, remember?

—and peeked through the screen.

"Shit!"

Diane would've fallen completely back into the room if not for the tight grip she had on the wooden framing around her window. Instead, she ducked her head down and pressed her face so tightly against the wall that she, momentarily, prevented any air from getting in through her nostrils.

No. No. No, no, no, no.

Someone was standing out at the end of her driveway. Right beside the trashcan she'd dragged out to the road before coming inside for the night. She hadn't made out any features—Eastham was known for not having much in the way of streetlights, particularly down many of the side roads and smaller neighborhoods—but she had seen the *shape*. The form of someone. Standing there and looking right up at her.

Oh, come on Diane. If you can't see his face, how do you know he's looking at you?

She thought a moment.

How do you even know it's a "he"?

Her grip on the windowsill tightened and her knuckles turned white. She nodded, convincing herself she needed to know, needed to check to see if she'd imagined it all.

You know, most likely—after all is said and done—you're gonna look back down there only to find it was actually a shadow from a tree or—

She couldn't come up with another possibility.

You have to look again, Diane.

Carefully she rose back up, just high enough to allow her eyes to peek again through the small opening.

It was gone. The shape. There was nothing behind the trashcan. Not even a shadow.

"Somehow that's even worse," she hissed. "That means someone *was* there and now—" she stopped herself from finishing the sentence. Without another thought, she dove back toward the bed and lifted the receiver off her Garfield telephone.

Chapter Eleven

Milty Burkitts

PLAY ▷

19 Clamneck Circle

MILTY HAD JUST FALLEN asleep. The issue of *Fangoria* he'd been reading was open over his face and, when the phone rang, he swatted the magazine onto the floor.

"Ah. H-hello?" he whispered groggily into the mouthpiece. He rubbed his eyes and looked toward his bedroom door, wondering if his parents had been woken. Though he did have a separate phone line—*quite a big deal* his Dad made a regular point of reminding him—the ring was loud and his folks were still likely to complain if he took calls at odd hours. "Who's—?"

"Milty?" Diane breathed so quietly on the other end of the line that he almost couldn't hear her.

"Yeah, it's me. Who—who is—?"

"Shut up. Just listen. It's Diane."

"W-why are you calling me? It's—" he started to look for his clock to figure out what time it was, but Diane interrupted him.

"Listen to me. Someone was outside. My window. Down by the street. Just standing there and looking up at me and I think it might be—"

"Woah, woah. Hold on. You're calling me because you saw someone? Outside?"

She sighed but there was a bit of a whine to it. "I think it might be...*him?*"

Milty scratched at his forehead and then saw what time it was. Just after ten, not as late as he'd thought. "It might be...*who*? You mean, *Rex*? Is that who you think it is? He's just an asshole, Diane, I wouldn't worry about—"

"No!" she snapped and then seemed to catch herself and lower her voice again. "No, Milty. Not Rex. I'm afraid—I'm afraid it might be the—"

"The *what*, Diane?

"*The Buoygeist.*"

Milty closed his eyes. He had a headache coming on. Too many beers and not enough water that night. It happened every time to him. Like clockwork. "Ah, shit. Diane...really? Look, I know tonight was a lot and we all got a little freaked out—"

"Milty."

He waited. She didn't continue. "Yes?"

"Please don't talk to me like I'm a child."

He sighed and dragged an open hand down the side of his face. "Okay, sure, sorry. *I'm sorry.* But—Diane, come on."

"No, you come on. Someone was standing outside my window—"

"Probably just Rex trying to scare you."

"*It wasn't Rex.*"

Milty stood up and stretched. He walked over to his window and let the phone cord drag on his matted, orange, shag carpet. "Tell you what. I'm gonna look outside now and—" and he peeked down at his front yard. "Yep. Nothing. Nada. No one's here, so—"

"Yeah, that's because it's over *here*, Dummy."

He let his shoulders hang.

I am so freaking tired. This is nuts. Just say something to calm her down.

"What can I do, Diane? I want to help, but—it's late and I'm pretty sure it was just Rex taking this whole thing too far. It honestly wouldn't surprise me if that's all this is, but—what do you need?"

Diane didn't hesitate. "Call Velma."

Milty felt his throat constrict. "Call—call *Velma*? W-why would I do that?"

"Uh, to see if she is okay? To see if Rex is there with her? Not exactly rocket science—"

"Well, I don't have her number, so—"

"Don't lie to me. I know you do. I *know* you've been holding on to that for years, waiting 'til you grew a pair and could convince yourself to just—"

"Okay, okay, *okay*," he put his hands up defensively, even though she couldn't see him. "Okay. I will call her. Jesus Christ."

Diane thanked him. "Please hurry. Call me right back."

"Yeah," he said. "Yeah, okay. Fine. Will do."

He hung up.

Unbelievable. So, this is going to be my first call to Velma? At this hour? Probably gonna wake up her dad and—

He reached into his side table and pulled out a worn copy of *The Hobbit*. Nestled inside the first few pages was a crumpled slip of yellow notebook paper with seven digits on it. A single number that he'd pulled—nearly a decade earlier—from the big phone book that lived on the kitchen counter downstairs.

Milty scrunched his face up, rolled his neck a few times, and exhaled.

Just get it over with.

He dialed.

The phone rang.

And rang.

And rang.

A voice answering machine clicked on. It was Velma's father's voice. "Green residence. We're not home. Leave a message after the beep and we'll call you back."

Beep.

Milty hung up before saying anything, then immediately dialed Diane's number from memory. They'd been calling each other since middle school, though never so late and never with such gravity.

Diane immediately answered. "Milty?"

"Ah, yeah. It's me."

"Well?"

He flopped back on his pillow and stared up at the ceiling. "No answer. I'm sure they're long asleep. Just as we should be."

Diane was silent. He could hear her breathing on the other end of the line.

"Diane?" he said. "You still there?"

She swallowed loudly into the receiver. "Milty, I'm scared."

"D-do you want to look out the window again? With me on the line?"

She agreed to do so and, after a few seconds, spoke again. "Nothing. There's nothing there."

Milty pulled his comforter over himself. "Okay, good. That's good. Look, I think—I think it's been a long night. I'm tired. You're tired. I'm sure it was nothing, Diane."

Again, she allowed for awkward silence as a response.

"Diane?"

"I'm—" she began, before deciding against saying whatever she was about to. "Okay."

He nodded. Relieved. "Okay. Well—"

"Can I call you again? You know, if—"

He was already starting to doze and yawned involuntarily. "Yeah, yeah of course."

"And you'll call me if—"

"I will. I promise."

He yawned again and thought maybe he'd heard her do the same.

"Okay, well. Thanks, Milty. 'Night."

His eyes were fully closed. "'Night, Diane."

Without looking, Milty returned the phone to its perch and pulled the string on his Frankenstein lamp.

Chapter Twelve

Velma Green

PLAY ▷

80 Fisherman Hollow Lane

THE METAL CHAIN ON the porch swing squeaked. Velma sat beside Rex with the back of her hand covering her mouth and nose. He was smoking a joint, and she never had been able to handle the smell. One of his legs was outstretched and his foot pushed off against the wrap-around railing. With each rebound, the chain cried out into the night.

He held the still-smoking nub out to her. "Want some?"

She shook her head and waved him away. "No, thanks," she said, folding her arms. It was starting to significantly cool off and they'd been sitting outside for at least an hour. She'd suggested they talk on the porch to avoid waking her parents. "Are you even going to answer my question?"

I've only asked you twice now.

He raised an eyebrow but didn't look at her. Then he shrugged. "What do you want me to say, Vel?"

She sucked the side of her mouth. "I dunno. I guess I mostly want you to tell me what was up with you tonight. And, shit, how 'bout saying you're sorry?"

He rolled his eyes. "Sorry?"

"Yeah, sorry. Sorry for ruining your night. Sorry for embarrassing you in front of your friends. Sorry for acting like a complete nutjob." He did look at her then. "Oh, that got your attention? Well, it's true,

Rex. You were so fixated on seeing the buoy tonight. It was—pretty intense. What was up with that?"

A muscle just under his eye twitched. "What do you mean?"

A bat flew across the sky and Velma watched it. It attached itself to a cupola on the roof of the house directly across the street. Without taking her eyes from it, she answered. "It was like you were in some sort of weird trance. Like—I dunno—you seemed *different*, somehow. Not your usual self."

He took a long toke of his joint. "Look, I'm sorry, Vel. I didn't mean to get all...*funky* tonight. Not sure what came over me. Maybe just—just got caught up in the moment."

She nodded. "Yeah. *Maybe*."

"You have to admit," he continued, "It's all pretty exciting. All this local legend stuff. I'm, like, really...*into it*."

She ignored that. It was one thing to be super "into" the lore of the town, but it was another thing entirely to get so completely consumed by it that you start disregarding the people around you—people you're supposed to care about, people you're supposed to be attentive to. And that wasn't all. There was something else. Something more disturbing about Rex's preoccupation with the buoy that evening. Something she couldn't quite put her finger on. He'd asked her about the stories on their way down to the Cape—a complete surprise—which could only mean that he'd known about them well before their trip and had waited until then to say anything.

But how? And why?

The chain whimpered under their combined weight again.

Creak, creak.

Rex took another deep drag before devolving into an elongated coughing fit.

Creak, creak.

"You okay there?" She put a hand on his shoulder and he nodded. "Take it easy, okay? Remember my parents are asleep."

She turned away from him and gasped.

Someone was standing under the lamppost at the end of the street.

In the middle of the road.

She whacked Rex in the leg. "Look."

His eyes were heavy, but he lifted his head. "Huh? What?"

She pointed. "Right there. Someone's there—I think *watching* us."

Rex leaned forward and squinted. "Huh. That's strange—gonna get hit by a car if he doesn't move. Can't see his face though. Just a silhouette. Big mother-f—"

"But who is it?" Velma was standing now with her back to the front door.

Rex hopped up and casually bounded down the steps of the porch before Velma could grab him. "Hey! Buddy! Hellooo there! Hey, can we help you?"

The figure didn't stir. Didn't respond. Didn't move in any way that suggested he—or she—had heard Rex's bellowed question at all.

"Shhh," Velma pleaded. "Rex, *don't*."

He was still walking down the stone path in the direction of the street but did make an effort to whisper back to her. "Sorry, I just wanna know who it is." He stepped out into the road and waved. "Hello. Sir? Can you hear me?"

Still, the figure didn't move. It was rigid. Frozen. Like someone had planted a massive scarecrow right in the middle of the road.

"Rex, let's go inside."

His eyes were still fixed on the shape. "I—just want a closer look."

"*Rex.*"

"Babe, chill.

"*Rex.*"

"Babe. Sunshine. It's—it's just some guy. Probably lost or—" he suddenly sounded less convinced. "—*something.*"

"I'm going inside. And I'm locking the door behind me. Come now or don't. I don't care anymore." She unlocked the door and saw that Rex was backing in her direction. He took one last look and then hurriedly stepped inside. Velma immediately latched and bolted the door behind them.

Rex flopped down on the couch. "So, you wanna watch a movie?"

Velma gestured outside. "What? Are you—? There's a strange man standing out there. And you just wanna—*watch a movie?*"

Rex got up and strode over to the window. He peeked through the blinds. "He's not even there anymore. I told you, it was just some guy and—"

Velma pushed him out of the way and looked outside.

Where did he go?

"I don't—"

"I told you. Guy was probably waiting for a taxi. It picked him up. Can you relax now?"

Velma held up a finger. "Don't."

Rex's mouth hung open and he cocked his head, visibly confused. "Huh?"

"*Don't* tell me to relax. *You* did all of this. *All* of this is your fault?"

Rex returned to the couch. He grabbed the remote and flicked the TV on. "I did all of *what* exactly?" Something suddenly dawned on him. "Don't tell me you think—oh, my God—wow, are you still on this Buoygeist stuff? Shit, Vel. You're so much better than that. Give me a break."

Velma stood in front of him. She put both hands on her hips. "Don't act like you don't believe this thing is real."

He shrugged. "You're nuts."

She laughed. "*I'm* nuts? You're the one who forced us out on the water tonight. Remember that? You're the one that just *had* to see it. And why? Why, Rex? What aren't you telling me?"

Rex Templeton cackled and put both hands behind his head. "Hey, Vel?"

She nearly spit on him. "What?"

"Boo!"

Velma stormed up the stairs. "You're *such* a dick. You can sleep down here. I'm going to bed."

He lifted both arms. "Aw, come on, Vel. It was a joke."

"Goodnight."

"Aw, Vel. Come on."

She slammed her door, not caring how much noise she made. Before jumping right under the covers, she ran to her bedroom window and looked down the street again. She found the lamppost, but there was nothing else there.

You're losing it, Velma. Time for bed.

She could hear the TV blaring in the room below her. *We'll deal with that in the morning.*

CHAPTER THIRTEEN

KYLE CROWELL

PLAY ▷

Kyle's Mom's Minivan

DALE AND BEATRIX WERE passed out in the back. Kyle looked at them through the rearview mirror and swore.

How do I always end up the chauffeur?

He gripped the purple, faux-suede cover his mother had added to the steering wheel.

All because my mom lets us use her van.

He shook his head.

A blessing and a curse.

A weird rattle emanated from under the hood and he barely registered a reaction.

But, mostly, just a curse.

"Dude, your mom's car is a piece of shit."

Kyle didn't take his eyes off the road. It was super late, super dark, and he was hours beyond tired. The other two hadn't wanted to go straight home after the weirdness at the marina and had begged Kyle to "just drive around for a bit". Listening to tunes. It was their typical shtick. And, normally, he would have been totally game—his mom's collection of 8-tracks was surprisingly extensive *and* impressive—but this particular evening had turned into a non-stop make-out fest for his passengers and he'd already reached his daily limit on gratuitous tomfoolery hours earlier. His patience was evaporating by the second.

"Oh—so you're awake, I see? Wonderful. Can we go home now or would you prefer I continue chaperoning the two of you until you've conceived your firstborn?"

Dale snorted. "Oh, har, har. You are *hilarious*. The next Rodney Dangerfield."

A red traffic light appeared ahead and Kyle gently tapped at the breaks. They squealed and he winced. "Christ, Mom."

Dale kicked the back of the driver's seat. "She needs to get those looked at, Brotha."

Kyle raised his eyebrows knowingly. "I keep telling her, but she's... *busy*."

Beatrix groaned slightly.

Kyle looked in the rearview again while they were stopped. "Is B okay?"

Dale didn't investigate. "Probably? Yeah, uh—she's breathing. I guess the peppermint schnapps did it for her tonight, after all. The lightweight."

Kyle laughed as the light turned green and he hit the gas without looking.

"Holy shit!"

He slammed on the brakes, nearly standing up in the process. His head grazed the ceiling and he leaned forward.

"What?" Dale yelled from the back. "You see a deer in the road or—?"

"I-I-I thought—hold on," Kyle frantically wiped at the fogged windshield. "Goddamn defrost not working for shit."

"Dude, did you *see* something?"

He moved his palm back and forth until he could get a clear view of what'd caused him to stop so suddenly. "Oh, *fuck*."

"What is it? Did you—?" Dale leaned forward between the two front seats and stopped speaking when he saw what'd caused Kyle to cuss.

"Who...is...*that*?"

A person was standing in the road. Or, at least, Kyle *thought* it was a person. The headlights from his mom's van only reached halfway up the figure, who—despite his upper torso being hidden—must have been enormous. Of what was visible, they could only see blackened, torn fabric that hung roughly to the person's knees. Its legs and feet were emaciated, scabbed over, and glistening. Its skeletal toes, in the places where flesh remained, were covered in boils, festering sores, and—

"Do you see that or am I—?" Dale's finger was pointed straight ahead.

"Yes," Kyle gulped and blinked a few times, realizing that he wasn't imagining the apparition and that the couple of beers he'd downed weren't to blame. "Yeah, I see it too. He's not touching the ground."

The figure was hovering about a foot above the blacktop. Kyle wondered if it was an optical illusion—like when you see waves over the pavement on a super-hot summer day—but quickly decided that was not the case.

"Hey. Hey—sit back." He fumbled to put the car into gear without removing his gaze. "We're leaving and—and then we'll—"

"Hold on a sec." Dale opened the sliding door and stepped out.

Kyle couldn't stop him. That Dale had exited the vehicle wasn't even fully processing, was barely registering. "Huh? Shit, Dale. Get back here," Kyle whispered. He looked out the windshield and the thing hadn't moved. "Now, man. Don't be stupid. Come on."

Dale held a finger to his lips without turning to Kyle and then took a couple of steps toward the front of the van.

"Uh, hi? Hello? Who's there? This—uh—this isn't funny, whoever you are."

Kyle reached over and rolled down the passenger side window. "*Dale.* Stop messing around. Get your ass back in the car, *now.*"

Again, Dale disregarded Kyle's pleading. "Look, man. You're standing in the middle of the road, in the middle of the night. You okay or—or are you tryin' to get yourself killed?"

Still, whoever it was didn't speak. Didn't move. Didn't *anything.* Dale took another step forward.

Kyle sat back against the seat and drummed his fingers anxiously. *Come on, come on, come on. This isn't right.*

He could see Dale standing awkwardly. His hands were on his hips, like someone's dad getting ready to lecture the kids in his basement for stealing drinks from his liquor cabinet. His physicality suggested, to Kyle, that he was trying to project some sort of authority over the situation. Some sort of tough-guy, macho, hand on my oversized belt-buckle sort of thing. "Look, Pal. You need to move it or lose it, alright? Get lost. You're blocking traffic."

The thing moved then. Slowly, it glided toward Dale and the front of the van. Dale put his hands up in front of himself as he was gradually gifted a closer look at the being. Kyle's view was still slightly shielded by a blind spot on the vehicle and by the unsympathetic shadows that meandered, unimpeded by the late hour.

"W-w-woah," Kyle could hear Dale stammering. "Hey, s-stop. Stop right there, mister. D-don't come any closer."

"Kyle, get in the van!"

At first, it looked like Dale was going to hold his ground but, as the shadow descended on him, he stumbled backward. There was a flash of something, a glint of metal that caught in the headlights, and Kyle saw a spear—*a harpoon*—skewer one of Dale's extended hands and then continue onward until it passed directly through his stomach and out the other side.

"*Shit!*" Kyle threw himself backward, nearly knocking open the driver's-side door. Blood had splattered into the open window and covered his otherwise ashen face.

Outside, Dale made a sound that reminded Kyle of the time his aunt had stepped on a frog, out on the lawn one morning, in her bare feet. The poor thing had exploded that day and made a wet plop of a cry before she'd run screaming back into the house. That was the noise that emanated from Dale's lips right before the spear was wrenched free of him. His eyes were already glazed over as he fell lifelessly forward into the road.

"Oh, no. Oh, no. Oh, shit. Oh, holy shit!" Kyle screeched, fumbling with the stick in an attempt to shift gears.

Beatrix had woken up just then, realized that she was covered in reddish bits of her boyfriend, and also started screaming. Kyle, without bothering to shut the sliding door, hit the gas. At some point, he must have unintentionally put the car in reverse because—as he stepped on the accelerator—the minivan careened backward into a nearby street sign.

What—?

For a brief moment, Kyle sat there stunned. Beatrix was still screaming—not anything intelligible, just pure unadulterated, visceral blubbering—and, eventually, she woke Kyle from his temporary stupor. B's hands were shaking his shoulders and he had to push her away, into the back seat, so that he could steady himself and focus on what was moving up the street toward them.

"Whaaaat issss thaaaaat?" Beatrix finally used actual words. "Daaaaaaaaale. It killlled Daaaaale."

The thing was walking—no, *floating*—calmly toward them. One of its arms was raised and Kyle could distinctly see the harpoon, even as the specter left the minimal illumination provided at the traffic stop and was largely cloaked in shadow. Kyle squinted and tried to get a look at the thing's face, but it was shrouded in a thin, wet hood. The only visible features were its gray, dried-out smile—its shriveled lips reminding Kyle of two dead worms—and a bit of exposed bone on its chin.

"Sit down," Kyle said, again pushing Beatrix into her seat. "Time to go." The van was smoking, but he was able to put it into drive and slammed on the gas. Kyle's mom's minivan whinnied and bucked—but did manage to finally lurch forward. He turned the wheel so that they were driving in the opposite direction from the creature—and Dale Fenton's still-bleeding corpse—and sped away into a nightmare that Kyle feared was only just beginning.

CHAPTER FOURTEEN

MILTY BURKITTS

PLAY ▷

19 Clamneck Circle

MILTY HEARD THE SQUEALING brakes and the slam of a car door only seconds before the pounding at the front entryway of the house. He'd just fallen asleep—albeit a shallow, barely-asleep, sleep—and the ruckus outside woke him easily. He fell out of his bed. Without much thought, his body responded to the late-night summons automatically, absent any sort of caution from his, presumably dozing, inner guide—a voice that, under normal circumstances, would have given him pause.

What...is...that...?

He bounded down the staircase, only thinking to stop the noise before it woke his parents, and regained full consciousness just as he slid the bolt and swung open the door.

"*Milty!*" Kyle pushed past him into the house, dragging Beatrix by the hand as he did so. She was openly weeping, with snot leaking from her nose, and Kyle could barely catch his breath. "Milty, it's—it's—"

"Shhh. Hold up. Hold on." He whispered hoping they would follow suit. "Shhh, my parents are asleep. It's the middle of the night guys. What is going—?"

Kyle squatted down on the hardwood floor, his face in his hands. He was moaning and rambling on about Dale and something to do with the road. It was hard for Milty to make sense of any of what he said. Beatrix sat down in a foyer chair—the one with the nail-head trim that his parents had been gifted on their wedding day—and cried.

"Guys," Milty tried again. "Start over. Take a breath and then will someone *please* tell me what the hell is going on?"

Kyle gulped and seemed to visibly attempt to steady himself by placing both of his palms flat on the floor. He breathed in through his nose and out his mouth a couple of times before speaking. "Milty—it's Dale, he's—"

"*DEAD!*" Beatrix wailed and dropped her head backward onto the chair.

Milty felt a shiver run down his spine and he leaned on the wall. "What? *Dead?* W-what do you mean? How—how is he dead? What happened?"

Kyle stood up and grabbed Milty's upper arms. He squeezed hard, perhaps not fully aware of what he was doing. His eyes were bloodshot, and he had a red stain dripping down one of his cheeks and onto his neck. "Milty, just listen to me. It's happened. It's—it's *happened*, Milty. It's *here*."

Milty shook Kyle's grip off. Beatrix was still sobbing and he knelt beside her. "What are you *talking* about? You aren't making any sense. How many more beers did you have after you left?" Kyle was still rambling and Milty tried to talk over him. "Okay, slow down for a second. What's happened? What's *here*?"

Kyle wiped at his eyes furiously. "Don't you get it? You're not *list-en-ing*," he dramatically emphasized every syllable of the word. "How do you not understand? You were there—at the marina. We did this. It's the *Buoygeist*. We brought this on ourselves and now—now, it's here. It's come for us. Just as we knew it would. *It's come for us*."

Milty closed his eyes and rubbed at a freshly forming headache. "No. *No.* That's not—no way." He clasped his hands over his head, trying to sort everything out. "I'm sure there's more to whatever you saw tonight. I mean, there's got to be—it's not real, Kyle. Right? It can't be. It's insane to think—I mean, how could—?"

"*It's real.* I saw it. B saw it too. Which means someone, one of us, must have *wanted* it. One of us called to it. And it answered."

"Oh, come on. You can't expect me to—" Milty eyed the red substance that dappled Kyle's face. "And Dale?"

Kyle trembled, and flecks of spittle sprayed as he spoke. "It *killed* him, Milty. I watched it happen. It—it took its fucking harpoon and—"

Beatrix bellowed then and Milty threw a hand over her mouth. "Shhh, shhh. Please. Okay, I'm sure—it must be—there must be some kind of explanation. There *has* to be. It's a—a prank, right? Dale's messing with you both? Or—*something*? He's got to be. That sounds just like him and I bet—I bet he was—"

Kyle growled. "Oh, go to Hell, Milty. Go right to Hell. I'm telling you, this thing is real. And this all really happened. We saw it. Dale's dead, like *dead*-dead, and you need to stop trying to explain it all away. It *happened*."

Milty pulled Beatrix in for a hug after she started wailing again. "It just seems so hard to believe, guys. I—"

"Milty!" Beatrix had turned on him, but—before she could say anything else—he squeezed her even tighter and she dropped her face into his shoulder.

He swallowed. "Alright. *Alright.* We're gonna figure this out, but first—first we need to call Diane. She said she saw something outside her house too. The first thing we need to do is make sure she's alright. Make sure that—whatever thing you saw—isn't coming for her next. Then we'll go get her." He looked up the staircase. "Stay here. Don't go anywhere. I'll be right back."

Kyle dropped down beside Beatrix. "Hurry."

Milty ran back up the stairs to his bedroom. He picked up his phone and dialed.

Diane answered before the second ring. Evidently, she hadn't gone to sleep. "Hello?"

"Diane? Are you ok?"

"Yes, I'm—what's wrong? You sound...*wrong*."

Milty rubbed a bit of sleep out of his eyes. "Get dressed. We're coming to get you."

Diane gasped. "Wait, who's—?"

"I'll explain when we get there. Just be ready. See you in ten."

Milty smashed the phone down and then swapped his pjs out for the same pair of shorts he'd been wearing earlier that evening. He grabbed his flip-flops, ran for the stairwell, and snatched his hat off the post at the bottom.

We'll just get to Diane and then we'll figure this all out.

Kyle and Beatrix were standing and waiting when he got to them.

There's got to be an answer for this. I'm sure it can't be what they think it is.

Milty grabbed the door and pulled it open. The other two followed him back outside.

It just can't be.

CHAPTER FIFTEEN

DIANE SHAW

PLAY ▷

103 Barnacle Cove Road

Someone else saw it too.

Diane was dressed and waiting.

And something's happened. Milty wouldn't be on his way otherwise. "We're coming to get you." Who's we?

As she sat on the ledge of the bay window in her living room, Diane put on her foam Drive-In cap and pulled her ponytail out the back. A few minutes earlier, she'd quickly fished her clothing from that evening—still carrying a lingering campfire smoke aroma—out of the laundry basket and hastily jotted down a note for her parents on an index card. She stuck it on the fridge under a Dan's Lobster House magnet. It read, "Gone for the night. Be back in the morning." Diane was twenty-one and didn't need to leave them any notice at all, but she didn't want to risk them getting worried and deciding to go look for her.

If I'm right—and I know I am—someone else saw it. It's stalking us. Every single one of us who was at the marina tonight.

She chewed her bottom lip, deep in thought.

But no one else needs to be involved. No one else needs to see it. No one else needs to put themselves in harm's way. Only the seven of us. It's only after the seven of us. For now.

She hoped she was right. Her theory, in its entirety, was based on the story they'd grown up with.

As long as everyone else stays out of its way, they—at least—should be fine.

As she looked back out the window, a minivan—instantly recognizable as Kyle Crowell's mom's—pulled into her driveway. She hurried to the front door and opened it, just as three disconcerted faces appeared out of the night.

"What's going on?" she said. "What's happened?"

They all pushed past her. Kyle pointed at the door. "Shut it."

"What?"

"I said, shut it, Diane. Shut the door. Now."

She did what she was told and then took stock of the other three. Milty had his hands over his own trucker hat, his curls billowing out the sides—*so cute*—Kyle was pacing back and forth and muttering something rapidly under his breath, while Beatrix shivered in a corner. Long rivulets of tears dried on her face, mascara smeared, her big hair somehow even bigger. Diane looked around, realizing right then that someone was missing.

"Where's Dale?"

Milty pointed at the couch. "Why don't we all just sit down, take a minute, and—"

Beatrix wrapped her arms around Diane and whimpered. "He's dead, Diane."

No.

"What? How?" She looked over Beatrix's shoulder at the other two. Milty pointed to the living room again, but Kyle started ranting.

"It's here, Diane. Milty said you saw it too. It's—it's definitely here. Just like the story warned us it would be. Someone must've—must've wanted it."

Her eyes enlarged, not questioning him. "And it got Dale?"

Kyle nodded. "I watched it happen."

Diane held tightly to Beatrix, whose sobs were getting louder again. "Wait. It actually worked? But, how? Who would—I mean, which of us—?"

Milty raised his voice then, trying to regain some control of the situation. "Why don't we all sit down and try to avoid jumping to any conclusions? Okay?" He gestured a third time toward the couch. "We don't know anything yet." Kyle scowled at him—they'd already hashed out multiple times with specificity what he and B had witnessed with their own eyes. "Fine, *almost* nothing."

Diane helped Beatrix into a loveseat and the other girl immediately curled into the fetal position. Diane squeezed in beside her and—once Milty and Kyle had taken seats opposite them, over on the couch—spoke. "Tell me everything," she said.

And Kyle did.

Diane listened, leaning into and reacting animatedly to each aspect of the tale. When he'd finished, she reclined with her hands behind her head, considering the ceiling. "It's interesting. I guess, somebody wanted him. If this is all real, I mean. That's the only way it'd work, right? But, *who*?"

Milty, who'd been lying back with his eyes closed, flew forward as if he'd suddenly been woken by a rather large crack of thunder. "Oh, come on, Diane...not you too?"

Not me too? Are you blind? Did you even hear what Kyle just said?

She took a breath and tried out a measured response. "It's the only thing that makes sense, right?"

Milty shook his head. "Wrong. There are probably like, *a million* explanations for this. Someone playing a prank, maybe someone—like, a real-life *human*—is responsible for whatever happened to Dale. Who the hell knows? But that certainly doesn't mean it's some...*demon* that—what—*lives inside a buoy*? Do you know how insane that sounds, Diane?"

She was surprised at how much his directness, and his framing of the situation, hurt her. The way he was looking at her, she could tell he was questioning her sanity. That the harsh assessment was coming from him—her chronically unrequited crush—made Diane feel immediately nauseous. But, despite all of that, she stood her ground and lifted her chin.

"It doesn't matter what you think, *Milty*. I believe what *I* saw a little while ago. I believe Kyle now—B saw it too—and I believed the story when we told it to Rex out on the marina tonight." She massaged the headache that was building in her forehead. "We should never have told him. *I* should never have told him."

Milty grabbed a throw pillow and held it to his face. He screamed a muffled scream into it.

Diane ignored him. "Do whatever you gotta do to make yourself feel better, but it's not changing anything. We—all of us, everyone who was there tonight—are in danger. And, if we're going to survive to the morning, we need to—"

There was a loud *thwump* far above their heads.

Kyle was already standing. Milty pulled the pillow off of his face. "Was that your parents? Falling out of bed or—?"

Diane shook her head, staring up. "No way. That—that sound didn't come from upstairs."

"Okaaaay. Then, where—?"

"The roof," she gulped. "Something's on the roof."

Thwump. The same sound again, but a little louder.

"Should we go get your parents?" Beatrix was sitting up straight.

"No," Diane whispered, her head cocked so her ear was pointed upward. Listening. "They're not here. Away for the weekend. And, even if they were home, I wouldn't want them to wake up and see it because—"

"Because then they'd be part of it too," Kyle finished.

"Right."

Milty looked at the other three. "This is crazy, seriously crazy. You *do* acknowledge that?"

Diane stood up and gently took Beatrix by the hand. The two started walking toward the door. "Fine. Let's be crazy together then."

Kyle followed her, but Milty remained seated.

"What do you mean? Diane? Hold up. Where are you—?"

Thwump. Again. Louder.

"It's here," she said, locking eyes with him, pleading. "And we need to leave. *Now.*"

CHAPTER SIXTEEN

MILTY BURKITTS

PLAY ▷

Kyle's Mom's Minivan

THAT'S—THAT'S NOT POSSIBLE.

Milty couldn't take his eyes away from the roof of Diane's house as Kyle backed out of the driveway. He rode shotgun, while Diane cared for Beatrix on the bench seat behind them. Milty leaned forward, unaware of how wide his mouth was hanging.

What...is...that?

"Do you see it?" Kyle said as he turned the wheel and accelerated up Barnacle Cove Road.

Milty nodded, but the gesture was disembodied from what currently raced through his brain. On the Shaw roof, just beside the chimney, was a colossal shape—humanoid, *sure*, but larger than any person he'd ever seen in real life or otherwise. The night was darker than most, undoubtedly overcast with clouds that dawdled and blocked the moon even though they couldn't be seen. The figure—whatever it was—towered above the tallest of the neighborhood trees, largely ill-defined and, in places, somewhat amorphous. Vaguely a shadow, the thing was—even more nebulously—an indisputable being of some concrete, physical substance. The shape was characterless in moments and yet, as it twitched and then glided—tracking their movement as it leapt from one roof to the next—folds of a muddied, silk-like fabric flapped and danced in an impossible, invisible dream-breeze. Its vestment was

charred in places, shredded in others, and glistened—dripping and
saturated in a caliginous sludge that could only have originated in the
most lifeless, most execrable depths of the ocean's floor.

"Diane—?" Milty said, turning around. He didn't know what he
wanted to ask her, but she understood just the same.

"I see it," she said. "It's *him*."

The minivan was picking up speed. Milty faced the passenger
window again and then—then he saw it staring back at him.

Ho-ly—

Though it still kept pace with the van, effortlessly bounding from
rooftop to rooftop in the tightly packed neighborhood, its head was
now turned grotesquely sideways—fixed so that the creature's face
was focused directly onto them and, more specifically, right at Milty.
Nearly retching at the sight, Milty covered his mouth. Mummified
skin the color of beef jerky, pickled by centuries of hibernation at the
bottom of the Atlantic, stretched tightly over the villain's skull. Its
eye holes were vacant caverns that offered shelter to only a few stray
slivers of decaying algae and its jaw drooped involuntarily, leaving just
a wide enough gap for a rotted stub of a tongue to slither in and out
in synchronization with each vault the demon took.

Oh my God.

Milty felt Diane reach out and squeeze his elbow. He grabbed her
hand in return. "I'm sorry," he said. "For not believing you. I should
have—"

She grabbed his chin and turned him to look at her. "It's okay.
I understand. How *could* anyone believe something like this? But,
unless we're all sharing in some massive group hallucination—"

He closed his eyes. "I know, I—" he was looking back out
the window again. "Hey, wait. Wait, it's—it's gone. I don't see it
anymore."

They all strained to peer into the gloom. Kyle started to brake,
but Milty urged him to keep going. "Don't stop. I don't care that we
don't see it. It's still out there. Somewhere. Just keep moving."

Kyle did as he was told. "So, uh—we got a particular destination
in mind? Or am I just driving around aimlessly?"

Milty watched as Diane ran her fingers through Beatrix's long, dark, poofed-out mane. He thought B looked like she was asleep. "What do *you* think, Diane?"

Again, she chewed on her lip. Milty'd noticed she did that whenever she was deep in thought and, as he recognized she was doing it once more, found himself staring perhaps too long at her mouth and at the little twitch her nostrils made as she settled some sort of internal debate.

Focus, Milty.

She caught him gawking at her, a half-smile knowingly, briefly, crossing her lips. "You good?"

He blinked twice. "I—*yeah*, I—I guess thought you would have an idea where we should go. Kyle's right. We can't just drive around all night."

She looked down at Beatrix. "No. We can't." She leaned forward, bringing her face near the side of Kyle's head. "You know how to get to Velma's house, right?"

Kyle scoffed. "Of course."

Milty squinted at her. "Velma's?"

Diane nodded. "Well, yeah. If this thing's after us, it's after her and Rex too. Right? Makes sense we all stick together. If nothing else, we need to warn them."

"If they're even alive." It was Beatrix. She sniffed a couple of times and, although she hadn't opened her eyes, offered them all a new, grim, fatalistic possibility to consider.

Milty's grip on Diane's hand—and hers on his elbow—suddenly felt of far greater consequence.

If they're even alive.

CHAPTER SEVENTEEN

VELMA GREEN

PLAY ▷

80 Fisherman Hollow Lane

"REX," VELMA HISSED FROM the top of the staircase, taking great pains not to wake her sleeping parents. "Rex. Are you going to answer that?"

Someone had knocked on the front door. In the middle of the night. It was a light, frenetic tap. Quiet, but persistent. It'd lasted at least a few minutes—long enough for her to stumble out of bed and look over the balcony. Rex was asleep with the TV still on. Since it was the middle of the night, whatever he'd been watching was now only static.

"Hey," she whispered. "You awake?"

He didn't stir. She sighed and tiptoed down the stairs.

You should have peeked out the window first.

A little voice sprung forth in her head. The warning, she knew, was justified. The more she thought about it, the more panicked she became.

Who is knocking on our door in the middle of the night?

Velma looked through the peephole.

Immediately she made out four people, dark shapes at that hour, standing on the front steps. The shark-fin on the first sweatshirt told her that one of them was Milty. Perplexed, she cracked the door and poked her head out.

"Uh, hey guys. What's—?"

"Can we come in?" Milty's lips were pressed together. He looked pale.

"I—uh, it's kinda late. My parents—"

"It's important." It was Diane, leaning out from behind Milty.

Velma acquiesced. "Okay, just—please be quiet. My parents are asleep."

They filed in.

Milty. Diane. Kyle. And...B?

'Would someone please tell me what's going on?"

"Where's Rex?" Milty was looking around.

"Why? What do you—?"

Rex walked in from the living room scratching his bare stomach. "Heyo, party's here. 'Sup bros." He held up his hand, looking for a "high-five".

Milty ignored him. "You both need to come with us."

Something's wrong.

"Come with you? Why? Wait, where's Dale?"

Kyle looked about ready to scream. "We'll tell you in the car. But you need to come *now*."

Velma looked at the four faces that'd awakened her. They were a bedraggled lot, tears staining more than one set of cheeks, and each of them had giant bags under their eyes—illustrative of how little sleep they'd all had.

"Vel," Beatrix's mouth was quivering. "Dale's dead."

Dead? What was that word again? Velma felt her face and her arms go numb. What B said wasn't registering, didn't make any sense. The room began to spin a bit and some combination of both Milty and Rex caught her. "How?" was all she could muster.

Milty put an arm around her awkwardly and Rex lifted an eyebrow. "We will tell you in the car." He tried to get Velma's eyes to meet his, but she was staring off elsewhere. "Hey. Please. You need to come with us. Grab whatever you need. Get some shoes and then we gotta go."

She started to refocus. "But—my parents. We need to—"

Diane came nearly nose to nose with her. "They *can't* know. It's *safer* for them *not* to know. Trust me."

Trust you?

Nothing made any sense, but Velma did as they told her. In her room again, she quickly changed out of her pajamas and found a pair of tennis shoes. It wasn't incredibly cold, but she grabbed a fleece headband as she exited back into the upstairs hallway. Passing by her parent's bedroom, she stopped and pictured the two of them blissfully unaware and slumbering away. And then—right then, in that moment—she committed to *trusting* her friends, even though they'd told her so very little up to that point. Even though they still hadn't said what was going on.

Trust.

Velma blew a kiss to her mom and sent a second one to her dad.

It's safer for them not to know.

Chapter Eighteen

Kyle Crowell

PLAY ▷

Kyle's Mom's Minivan

LET'S GO, GUYS. WHAT'S the holdup?

Kyle was in the driver's seat with the engine running. Velma had run upstairs to change and the rest of them were lingering inside waiting for her. Kyle, getting antsy, had run out ahead of them.

Come on, come on.

The front door of the house opened and a small windchime of a pink lobster clinked, fighting against a sudden gust of salty air. It waved an oversized claw at Kyle and he shuddered. Milty and Diane were down the steps first. Rex was next, followed by Velma. Beatrix was lagging behind them all, her eyes glossed over, still stumbling around in a partial daze.

Come on.

Diane hopped in the passenger seat this time and Milty took a seat directly behind Kyle. Rex made his way to the back row.

"Oh, well wouldja look at this? It's the party bus." Rex flashed devil horns as he got in, but even he didn't sound like he was having fun anymore.

Come on, you two, what's taking so long?

Velma was a few steps from the van, whispering something to Beatrix. The other was crying again, and Velma ran a hand up and down her back while, at the same time, coaxing her toward the sliding door. Abruptly, Beatrix let out a high-pitched wail, pulled away from her friend, and threw her arms around a nearby lamppost. Velma followed and began attempting to pry her off of it.

"We got to go," Kyle said through gritted teeth. "Milty can you—?" He gestured toward the open door.

"Uh, yah—uh, hey, ladies—time's up. We gotta rock 'n roll—" He lost the last few words of what he'd been about to say. A shadow appeared from above the home's front walkway and cast a sooty pallor over everything the minimal light from the single lamppost touched. Kyle saw Velma's arms go slack and her mouth drop open wordlessly. She released her grip on Beatrix.

"Get in!" Kyle called to her. "*Now!*"

Velma screamed and stumbled toward the van. Milty stepped onto the sidewalk and reached for her hand, pulling her inside.

It's here.

Though Kyle couldn't see their assailant, he could hear the flapping of its soiled garment. A muffled cry emanated from Beatrix but stopped almost immediately as it'd begun.

The lamppost. Kyle strained to see into the night, in the direction the metal beacon. *She's—she was just there. She was just right there. Where'd she go?*

Only moments before, the unmarred light fixture had stood tall on the front lawn of the Green residence, but now—Kyle realized—it was bent completely sideways. The bulb at its precipice flickered and basked their surroundings in a strobe effect, making it nearly impossible to see clearly.

But, where—?

"B!" Velma lamented as she wildly searched for her friend. Milty had her wrist, preventing her from jumping back outside. A violent gust threw bits of sand and earth into their faces, temporarily blinding all of B's would-be rescuers. Before anyone had an opportunity to even question where she'd gone, Beatrix let out another scream—by the sound of it, from a significant distance off—far, *far* above their heads. And then, moments later, bits of something wet and juicy pelted the van's roof in gruesome, intermittent *plops.*

Like meaty drops of rain.

Kyle covered his ears, trying to prevent himself from hearing any more.

No.

"Where's is she?" Velma was trying to scramble back outside. Milty had his arms around her waist. "What *is* that? Where is she? B!"

"Shut the door!" Kyle screamed.

"I can't!" Milty struggled with Velma who was still trying to break free of him. "Rex, shut it!"

This time, Rex *was* helpful. He reached out and threw the slider closed.

"B!" Velma howled again.

Diane turned to Kyle. "Go, go, go, go! Drive!"

He blinked at her. "W-what about, B—?"

Diane glared at him and then forced Kyle's hand to put the car into gear.

"She's gone! Drive!"

The minivan's engine revved and Kyle drove away, his windshield wipers thwacking ineffectually back and forth at the unusually sloppy precipitation.

CHAPTER NINETEEN

MILTY BURKITTS

PLAY ▷

The Police Station

"HEY, EVERYONE, JUST SHUT the hell up. She's right."

Milty was standing beside Diane in front of the police station. The two of them were blocking the rest of their friends from entering. At first, he'd agreed with the others that they needed to seek help and some sort of shelter from the evil that currently pursued them. But Diane had made a convincing argument that involving anyone else would be selfish, unhelpful, and only put others in harm's way. *No one else needs to die tonight*, she'd insisted.

Milty put his hands up. Kyle, Rex, and Velma were just about to barrel past him and certainly would've been able to do so without much effort if that'd ended up being their ultimate decision. "Listen to me," he tried again. "Diane's right. If we bust in here and that thing follows us, then more people get involved and more people are gonna die. What're their guns gonna do against that thing anyway?"

Kyle tried to push by him and Milty got in front of him again. "Move your scrawny ass, Milty," Kyle said.

Milty shook his head. "Listen to me—"

"No, I'm done listening to anyone else," Kyle's voice was getting louder. "Dale and B are both dead. *Dead.* Those were my friends. I don't care what you say to me—"

"Kyle."

"—but I'm going in there."

He knocked past Milty easily and Diane threw herself on the glass entrance. Kyle was going to need to push her to the ground if he wanted to get by. "Hey. Stop. Think about this for a second."

"No."

"Kyle, just *listen*. What're they even going to do for you? Huh? You saw what it did to Dale and Beatrix. What could they possibly do—?"

He shook his head. Beads of perspiration flecked his forehead even with the brisk temperature that evening. "They can put me behind bars, is what they can do. For the night. Lock me up and throw away the key for all I fucking care. That thing's not getting at me in there."

Diane started to shake her head, but Velma jumped up next to him. "I think Kyle's right. A jail cell without windows might be just what we need to make it 'til morning. And that's all we need to do, right Diane? Survive until morning?"

She laughed uneasily. "I dunno. If you believe all of that, the stories I mean, then—maybe? Sure, I guess. But, who the hell knows? They're *stories*. Clearly based in *some* reality as we all now are well aware. But—" She closed her eyes. "It's not exactly like any survivors have lived to provide us with a 'How-To' guide. How could we *really* know? There's no certainty with any of this."

Maybe hiding out isn't such a bad idea?

The thought was fleeting and Milty swallowed it. He wanted to support Diane in that moment, but the idea of barricading themselves in some sort of prison fortress—he had to admit—did have its appeal.

"Diane," Velma said. "You're right. We don't know—well, *anything*. Except we *do* know that something is trying to kill us. *Out here*. Our safety might be in there. *Might* be. But I'm not waiting out here any longer. I'm not waiting to figure out if we can survive by just—frantically running around town all night. We need to do *something*." She swallowed, getting ready to make her move. "And this is the only something I can think of right now."

With Kyle's help, Velma moved Diane out of the way. She only protested a little. The two of them hurried inside and Rex nonchalantly followed.

Diane was looking up at Milty, fear and dejection plastered across her face.

Don't let her stay out here by herself, you idiot.

"Come in with us. It's not safe outside."

Without a word, she obliged and he trailed after her. When they stepped into the station, Velma, Kyle, and Rex were already at the counter speaking with a police officer. Milty and Diane joined them mid-conversation.

"Woah, woah, woah, woah," the police officer said, holding his hands high, defensively. "Just—just calm down for a minute. I'm not really following any of what you kids are telling me and I'm currently dealing with a few more pressing things at the moment, thank you very much. Everyone else on duty just got called to a bad accident near Nauset Beach. I'm alone and—"

"Please," Velma interrupted the small, surprisingly frail-looking man. The name plate on his uniform read "Z. Barnsworth". "He wasn't elderly, by any means, but his cheeks were sunken in such a way that gave the appearance he'd not received sufficient sustenance in quite some time. His overall color was *gray*. The few wisps of hair on top of his head trembled and danced around as he gesticulated for them all to calm down.

"Now, look," he stammered. "I'm gonna have to ask the—how many of you are there—*five* of you to just take a seat over there and I'll—"

"Our friends are *dead*, you asshole," Kyle growled and leaned over the counter like he might try to bite the brittle little man.

Once more, the officer put up his hands as if someone had just pointed a gun at him.

Force of habit?

"Hold on. Dead, you say?"

"Yes," Velma cried, pounding her fists on the counter. "Goddammit, I've been trying to tell you—"

Screeeeeeeeeeeeeeeeeeeeeech.

Metal on glass. A slow, intentional drag. Near the front of the station. All heads turned in the direction of the noise.

The officer's hand immediately went to his holster. "I-I-I-Is that another one of your friends out there? This some sort of game? Tell me now. It's gettin' late and I don't have the time for any of this." He stepped out from behind the counter. "You all stay right here."

You have to stop him. Milty swatted absentmindedly at the voice.

"Officer, I think you should wait and listen to us—"

"N-n-no you listen to *me*, Son. You stay right where you are." The tiny man approached the glass door.

"Officer—"

"I told you to stay!"

Milty took a step in the man's direction, despite the warning. "Officer, this thing—"

The policeman held a finger to his mouth and kept it there. Peering outside, without opening the door, he pressed his ear firmly to the glass. After a moment, a large smile cracked on his anemic, haggard face. "Must have been a branch caught on the wind. I told them months ago that scrub pine was too close to the main entrance. Just a bit of wind and this is what happens. Predictable, but nothing to worry about. Besides, as far as I can tell, there's not a single living soul out there right now and—"

The glass shattered inward, spraying bits of translucent shrapnel into the station. A skeletal arm reached in and latched itself to the front of the officer's uniform. He yelped and tried to reach for his gun but was pulled out into the night before he could yelp a second time. Red smeared the human-sized hole that Officer Z. Barnsworth disappeared through.

Get them out of here. Go, now!

Milty grabbed Diane and started running. He didn't know where. Toward the back of the station. Toward another exit. Regardless, she ran with him and he sensed the others did too. No one spoke. There was nothing left to say. Stunned and barely feeling the shards sprinkled and embedded into their skin, they stumbled out—out again into the darkness—though Milty wasn't even fully aware of how they'd managed to do so.

Run.

The air was still crisp and their wounds from the glass implosion were numbed by the terror that bombarded and assailed them from all angles. Milty gasped for a breath but didn't think he'd ever stop moving, even if he ran out of air entirely.

Run, he coaxed himself. *Run and don't look back.*

Chapter Twenty

PLAY ▷

Kyle's Mom's Minivan

Jesus.

The van was already moving, though Milty had no memory of it ever leaving the side of the police station. Everyone sat in confused, astonished silence. In the rearview mirror, Milty could see that Kyle's lips were moving. He was mumbling to himself, his eyes fixed on the road ahead. A single bead of sweat hung suspended on the tip of his sunburned, peeling nose. Milty leaned forward and put a hand on his shoulder. Kyle jumped.

"What—?"

"Sorry, it's me. It's Milty. Didn't mean to scare you. I just—I just wanted to know where you were heading."

Kyle flinched. One of his eyes twitched, and he brought a hand to his face in response as if he were swatting at an invisible insect. "Dunno. Anywhere. Everywhere. Somewhere. What does it matter? We're all screwed either way, right?" His head swiveled back and forth, from one side of the car to the other. "Anywhere's better than..." He didn't need to finish the thought.

Milty sat back. Diane was beside him, while Velma and Rex occupied the row in the rear of the vehicle. Velma was weeping, though Rex didn't seem to be trying all that hard to console her. Instead, he was twirling one of his long, blonde dreadlocks as if he were on a leisurely Sunday drive to the surf shop. His head bopped to music that wasn't playing.

What a prick.

"Hey," Diane whispered, leaning toward Milty's ear. "Hey, we're starting to get closer to the center of town. We should get off this road. I—I think this is a bad idea."

Milty looked out the window. At some point, they'd made their way back onto Route 6—a main thoroughfare—and were headed toward some of the more crowded tourist spots. Even during the month of October, if you were looking for more human congestion, more people—*more bodies*—it was in that area you'd find them. Restaurants—half of them lobster-themed—little storefronts where beach chairs and gaudy inflatables could quickly be purchased, and other popular tourist traps, littered the roadside as they passed on by.

"Hey, Kyle, take a turn somewhere. We need to get off this road," Diane quietly pressed him before raising her voice a bit to be heard over the van's rather loud muffler. "Hey, uh, Kyle? You hearing me? We need to get off this road. Pick a side street, any side street, but this is...*not* the best place for us to be."

Kyle didn't respond. His lips continued to squirm and twitch. He was aggressively chewing on a flap of skin that dangled from the corner of his mouth.

Rex leaned forward and made a circular motion with a finger by the side of his head. "I think somebody's gone *by-by*."

Velma slapped him on the shoulder, but the concern on her face suggested she didn't disagree with Rex's sentiment.

"Uh, Kyle?" Milty attempted to get his attention. "You okay, Bud?"

Kyle nodded, but he didn't look okay. He didn't turn his head and didn't otherwise acknowledge that anyone was speaking to him.

"Kyle? Hey, man, why don't you—why don't you just go ahead and pull over for a second and—"

"I'm *fine*," he said through gritted teeth before making a second, more visible, more assuaging effort to convey his fine-ness. His jaw flexed as he put on an obviously fake smile. "I'm fine."

Yeah, Pal. Well, you definitely don't look fine.

"What can I do?" Milty said, loud enough so that only Diane could hear him. "Can't very well force him off the road."

She brought her mouth to his ear. "Well, at least it's late. Almost midnight. Most people around here are in bed at this hour. I can't imagine we'll find any—" She froze, a sudden realization creeping across her face. "Oh my God."

Kyle flicked on the van's blinker.

"What?" Milty said. "What is—?"

"The Drive-In," Diane said numbly. "Oh, my God, Milty. *The Drive-In.*"

"B-but there's no one there, it's almost—"

"It's the *double feature.*"

Milty scratched his head. "No, it'd be done by now, Diane. It's..." He looked at his watch.

She glared at him. "Third Friday of the month. *Remember?* It's a *late* showing. Doesn't even start until 9. Which means it... hasn't ended yet."

The van took a left.

Oh, no.

Milty leapt up front into the passenger seat. At first, he tried to persuade Kyle to turn around. "Kyle, Man. Stop the car. The Drive-In is packed. We—we can't bring that thing here. It's following us, remember? We have to—"

The farthest corner of Kyle's mouth twerked upward in an almost-smile. "There are so many cars here—"

"Yes, exactly!" Diane pleaded. "You need to—"

"So many cars he—he just might not see us. We can hide."

"No!" Milty tried to grab the steering wheel but Kyle backhanded him across the face. Milty flopped against the passenger window, momentarily stunned.

Kyle pressed on the accelerator as they approached the ticket window. The attendant held out a hand for their admission fee, but the minivan drove right by and busted through the small wooden barrier before it could be pulled up in time.

Oh, my God.

Kyle was gone. Gone, but still driving. Driving headlong into a sea of cars, lawn chairs, popcorn smells, and late-night moviegoers.

On the screen, *A Nightmare on Elm Street 3: Dream Warriors* held hundreds of rapt gazes. No one stirred or noticed the loud minivan chugging into their midst.

Or the shadow that tracked its prey from above.

The slaughterous demon descended over the packed parking lot and the preoccupied, unconcerned rows of sheep, as they stuffed their drowsy faces with concession stand poison.

Chapter Twenty-One

Diane Shaw

PLAY ▷

The Drive-In

KYLE TURNED THE MINIVAN into an empty spot, tucked somewhere in the middle of the lot, and turned the engine off. On one side of them, a family of five snoozed inside their own car—all but one little girl who watched the movie intently while the rest of her family slept, chewing one of her fingernails to the quick—and on the other side, an older couple sat in front of their Buick in two lawn chairs. Wrapped around the senior citizens was a large quilt with an alternating green and red pattern.

This is bad. This is bad. This is bad.

Diane tapped her right leg. No other sound emanated from within the van. Breaths were held and, other than the muffled hum of the movie that'd managed to reach their ears from the speakers in the surrounding vehicles, there was only silence. She was doing a bit of mental math, trying to calculate how many people could've been in attendance that night—based on how many of the rows looked to be filled. Her many nights spent working at concessions told her it was a busy night. Especially for October.

One hundred and fifty. At least. Shit.

Milty put his hand on her leg to stop it from bouncing. She jumped and then relaxed once she realized it was him. "You alright?" he whispered, the lines on his forehead broadcasting to Diane that he already knew the answer.

She gulped. "One hundred and fifty," she mumbled.

He turned to face her more fully. "Huh?"

Diane grabbed his hand where it lay on her knee and squeezed. "One hundred and fifty. *Ish.*"

"I don't—"

She rolled her eyes. "That's how many people I think could be here tonight. Come on, Dude. Stay with me."

He nodded, understanding. "Oh. So, not good."

Her eyes got wider and she inhaled deeply. "No. Not good *at all.*"

Kyle spun around, his finger over his lips. He mouthed. "Be quiet," to them before facing the front again.

Screw you, Kyle. Who told you it was okay to put all of these lives at risk?

Diane wanted to hit him. They shouldn't have been there. There were other places they could've decided to hide. Other places where they wouldn't have been putting innocent people unnecessarily in danger. Other places that were not—

Here. The Drive-In.

The group continued to sit in silence. There was an occasional shifting in the row behind her, just enough that she could tell Velma and Rex were still awake.

How could they not be? Not like anyone could sleep under these conditions.

And then, she wasn't sure exactly why she did it—perhaps it was the exhaustion brought on by an evening of being hunted by an evil ocean spirit, perhaps it was the long work week—but Diane let her head rest on Milty's shoulder. He tensed and, at first, she thought he might try to move away from her. But he didn't. In fact, after a very obvious tremor rippled through him, he dropped his cheek onto the back of her head, and together—for the briefest of moments—the two of them breathed in harmony. For an instant, they were somewhere else. Blissfully distracted by the other. Somewhere far, far away.

It only took this nightmare to bring us closer, she mused sarcastically. *Couldn't we have just—I dunno—tried out a normal date first?*

Despite their situation, she managed to smile at herself.

Such a comedian, Diane. If only you could use that charm to—

She didn't allow herself to finish the thought, or—rather—the scene developing outside got in the way of her doing so.

A silhouette had suddenly appeared behind the screen. Whatever it was blacked out much of the center of the movie. Considering the dimensions of the massive drive-in backdrop, whatever caused the shadow could only have been substantial in size itself.

"Guys—" Diane ducked down behind the driver's side chair. She held out her arm and pointed ahead needlessly. They all had, of course, already seen it.

"Everybody, just stay quiet for a minute," Milty said, sitting up again.

The silhouette raised two arms, which blocked out even more of the movie. The crowd—as more people were roused from their slumbers and became aware of the disruption—began to boo. It was a low rumble at first, but within seconds the chorus began to grow in volume and intensity. Someone near the front row tossed an empty bucket of popcorn, which fell to the earth long before it ever had a chance of impacting the white canvas.

"They think it's the projectionist," Diane hissed. "Oh no, they're going to—"

A single car horn beeped from somewhere behind them. It was quickly followed up with additional angry retorts from all over the lot.

No, no, no, no, no.

And, as the cacophony and the discord of what'd only moments earlier been a dozing audience grew in size, so did the featureless shape behind the screen. The figure's arms stretched out on either side of itself and immediately Diane identified the obvious outline of their pursuer's long, pointed, skewer.

No! Quiet! Stop, you morons!

Kyle covered his eyes comically, peeking through his spread fingers, like a child watching the part of the horror movie his parents had told him not to.

Milty gripped Diane's knee again, more tightly, and she returned the sentiment.

The angry voices and boos continued to grow louder.

Riiiiiiiiiiiiiiiiiiiiiiiiiiiiiiiiiiiiiiiiiiiiiip.

The Buoygeist's harpoon impaled the center of the screen, and the bloodthirsty phantasm pulled itself through, eviscerating the placidity of the audience's Friday night at the movies. The double feature—now completely disemboweled—floated lifelessly to the earth, and the screams followed soon after.

Car doors began to open. One by one. People started to run into the night, over roofs and over one another, flailing for an easy escape. Hot dogs and boxes of Milk Duds were tossed aside as parents grabbed the hands of their sleepy-eyed children, while others tugged on their dogs' leashes before their beloved pets could run yelping at the monster that floated out into the heart of the crowd.

Wake up, Diane. Move!

Diane reacted instinctively. She jumped over Milty and pulled open the slider. Without saying anything, she grabbed his hand and pulled him out into the darkness with her.

And the Buoygeist descended, its progress marked by bloodcurdling screeching and futile pleading for mercy as he mowed his way through the chaotic throng of fleshy, cinema-loving souls.

CHAPTER TWENTY-TWO

VELMA GREEN

PLAY ▷

The Drive-In Bathroom

VELMA CROUCHED ON THE toilet seat, making every effort to keep her feet off of the floor. She was entirely alone, having been separated from the other four in the confusion and pandemonium that immediately followed the demon's breach of the movie screen and its ensuing assault on the stunned moviegoers. She'd been the last to exit the minivan and had almost immediately been plowed over by a large, bearded guy in a purple and green tracksuit. In the brief instant she'd been able to focus on the man, she'd made note of how the parking lot lights reflected off of his slicked-back, greasy mane, and the large gold medallion that bounced up and down on his ample garden of chest hair. The medallion had somehow caught her right under the chin as he ran by and made her temporarily see stars. By the time she'd managed to regain her footing and allow her vision to refocus, her friends were all gone.

They left me.

She sniffed and reached for a hanging piece of toilet paper, which she then used to wipe her nose. She decided not to blow as she didn't want to draw any attention to herself.

Rex left me.

Somehow it hadn't surprised her, not that she knew for certain he'd abandoned her. *To be completely fair*, she thought, *he could have just lost sight of me. It was complete anarchy out there.*

At first, she hadn't known where to go. She'd tried searching the sea of terrified faces for any that she recognized but quickly came to understand that doing so was at her own peril. Not only had the likelihood of her being completely trampled increased with each passing second, but the malignant spirit itself was calmly heading straight for her. Or so he appeared to be. She witnessed, in a brief moment during which her knees locked and she became too petrified to move, the demon mowing through the crowd at an alarming and effortless clip. Gurgled cries for help were, on more than one occasion, accompanied by blanched, lifeless, corpses being tossed high into the air—the Buoygeist systematically emptying those unlucky folks, unable to avoid the snare of the creature's spear, of their crimson life source. The thing floated calmly along, leaving a wide path of viscera and carnage in its wake, and its feet—undoubtedly moldering and purulent under its begrimed, fraying cloak—never appeared. Never touched earth. Its sallow cheeks, covered in open sores that leaked a blackish sludge, were fixed permanently on the far reaches of its otherwise dehydrated visage, stuck in a never-ending smile.

When her knees finally unlocked, Velma had simply run to the first and only safety she could see.

The bathroom.

The small, red building was separated from nearly everything else. The concession stand and the ticket booth sat near the main entrance, while the bathroom was on the side of the parking lot opposite those two structures. Everyone else seemed, inexplicably, to be running toward the entrance or directly into the surrounding woods. But Velma quickly realized she wouldn't make it if she tried one of those routes. In almost every other direction, people fought one another for the right to escape, disregarding civility and any attempt at even feigning interest in the most basic precepts of human decency. Grandmas were being knocked to the ground. Frat boys home for the weekend were pushing past strollers with young children. All bets were undeniably off, and Velma decided to separate herself from the pack.

On top of the toilet seat, her legs pulled in tightly to her chest, she shivered. Her eyes were squeezed tightly shut, and she tried to replay the last image burned into her brain of the annihilative, cloaked monstrosity and the mayhem it'd unleashed. Just before she'd entered the bathroom, there'd been movement out of the corner of her eye.

Did it see me? Had it turned to watch as I entered through the bathroom door?

Velma was certain it hadn't.

She hugged her legs tighter.

Pretty certain.

The rusted metal doorway flung open then—smashing hard into the cracked cement wall and the poster reminding employees to "Wash Your Hands" before returning to work—and she immediately regretted her decision to barricade herself somewhere without an alternative means of escape. She put her hands behind her head and pressed her face into her knees.

Don't move, Vel. Don't move.

Something scampered inside, rubber soles squeaking on the grimy cement floor, and tumbled into the stall next to hers. She heard someone panting and immediately recognized that it was just another person deciding to take refuge in the tiny red shack. A voice spoke to her then, but Velma couldn't identify the owner of it.

"Hey," the person breathed heavily. "Hey, I saw you come in here."

Velma didn't respond. She didn't know who it was, nor did she feel it benefitted her in any way to answer.

"Hey," whoever it was tried again. "Look, I know you're there. You," he gulped. "You should know something."

"Shhh," Velma replied. "Just shut up, okay?"

She raised her head and saw the guy standing up on the toilet.

Is he trying to peek over at me?

Two bespectacled eyes looked down over the top of the barrier between the stalls. The teenager—Velma came to realize—had a messy, blonde shag on his head. "Hey," he whispered. "Hey—"

She glared up at him. "Shut up," she hissed.

The kid tried to climb a bit higher. "It's just that—that thing—it's—"

There was deafening *screeeeeeeeech* from outside. Metal on metal. Harpoon endblade on bathroom door. At the Drive-In. A typical Friday night on Cape Cod.

"It's here," the kid finally spat. "That's what I was trying to tell you. I'm really sorry. It *followed* me."

On cue, the door was torn from its hinges and—by the sound of it—tossed aside with ease.

Velma held her breath.

She was pretty sure the kid in the next stall did too.

Drip, drip, drip, drip.

The wet, pitter-patter of mucousy droplets told her that they were no longer unaccompanied.

Drip, drip, drip, drip.

The sound was closer.

Drip, drip, drip, drip.

Directly in front of the kid's stall.

Velma braced herself.

Drip, drip, drip, drip.

And then the kid started screaming. Pleading.

"N-n-n-no, p-p-please don't—"

Velma winced in anticipation.

There was a squishy sound.

Squish. Slosh. Slurp.

The kid babbled something unintelligible as fluid drained out his mouth, over his teeth and gums. Velma's eyes were trained on the top of the stall, and then she saw him lifted high, toward the ceiling. The kid's glasses crashed to the floor, and he stared at her. There were no words, but his eyes begged her to do something.

But there was nothing. Nothing she could possibly do for him.

Go, Velma. It's distracted. Now's your chance.

Velma got up, threw open the stall door, and sprinted outside.

Don't look, just go!

She couldn't see where she was headed, blinded by shock and guilt—her senses flooded with the syrupy purr that was the kid's last breath—but she willed her legs to keep moving.

CHAPTER TWENTY-THREE

MILTY BURKITTS

PLAY ▷

The Woods

"WHY DID WE STOP? Let's get the hell outta here, Man."

Milty rounded on Rex. Though he had very little muscle mass to speak of, the video store clerk was of above-average height and had a couple of inches on Mr. Drum Circle. Milty made an extra effort to stand at his most intimidating size. "You sonofabitch. You left her. Only thinking about your damn self and you just—you left Velma. *Your girlfriend.* Alone, somewhere back there and—and we're not going anywhere until we find her."

The four of them—Milty, Diane, Kyle, and Rex—stood at the edge of the parking lot, at the mouth of a small, dirt, footpath. It'd likely formed after decades of Drive-In attendees had traversed the wooded stretch, looking for a shortcut home late at night. The kids in Eastham simply called this sad plot of forest "The Woods", though it was made up only of tiny, woeful scrub pines—the kind of Cape Cod vegetation that thrived in the sandy, loose soil more than any other—and provided very little actual shelter or cloaking from what stalked them.

Doesn't matter. We're waiting for her.

The group squatted low to the ground, watching—from behind a small cluster of blueberry bushes—the bloody havoc currently being wreaked at the Drive-In. Moments earlier, the demon had disappeared into the lone bathroom at the center of the lot and, as far as any of them could tell, had not yet reemerged. But, in the aftermath of its gruesome passage from the movie screen to the restroom, there was only ruin. It'd left nothing else. Glistening shapes lay strewn across windshields, slumped over car speaker stands, and crumpled in the headlights of cars whose operators had made unsuccessful attempts to drive themselves out of the nightmare.

And he left her out there—that bastard.

Milty couldn't hide his sneer or the disdain he had for the other man. Though Rex could've just kept going—no one was stopping him—he'd stayed with the others. His reasons weren't immediately clear to Milty, who would've preferred the guy *not* stick with them. But Rex did stay, possibly because he too, somewhere down deep, wanted to wait for Velma—or, perhaps more believably, because he didn't know the area and was afraid of getting lost in the dark. He ran his hands along both sides of his head, smoothing his bleached, dried-out locks.

"I'm sorry," Rex said, almost sounding genuine in his regret. "I thought she was right with me. Right behind me, I mean. I swear. Wasn't until we got here that I noticed she was missing."

That's because you were only worried about yourself, you coward.

Milty did not say that part out loud. "Yeah, well..." he trailed off as his eyes met Diane's. They were soft, calming, and somehow he could tell she wanted him to just leave it alone.

Not worth it at this point.

Milty was the closest to the parking lot. Diane was right behind him, and both Rex and Kyle stood a good distance down the trail. Kyle, in particular, was almost invisible in the minimal shadow of the trees—just far enough from the light provided by the still-running projection of *Elm Street* that he, aside from an unsettling reflection bouncing off of his eyes, could barely be seen.

Milty was about to ask Kyle if he was okay when a face suddenly appeared at the end of the trail. Velma crashed into him and Diane caught the two of them before they hit the ground. Velma's face was tear-stained, with snot leaking down into her mouth, and her cheeks were a shade of red he'd never seen before. Her breathing was heavy and, at first, she couldn't speak.

"It's ok," he said to her. "You're okay now. Breathe. *Breathe.*"

Velma sobbed. Diane waved at Rex to come to them and he begrudgingly walked over.

"Hey, Babe," Rex said, nudging Milty out of the way. He hugged her. "You're okay. Oh, thank God. We waited for you. We knew you'd find us." He allowed his eyes to briefly latch onto Milty's glare.

Oh, you little piece of—

Diane, reading Milty's mind, grabbed his elbow and shook her head.

Velma sniffed and managed to finally speak. She looked up at Rex, an expression of disgust forming alongside a suddenly curled upper lip. She pushed off of him as she continued to collect herself, brushing futilely at some sort of dark substance on her sweatshirt. "I can't believe you. You just—"

"Babe," Rex said.

"—left me."

Bingo.

Rex tried to wrap himself around her again, but Velma extended her arms, creating more distance. "No, not now."

"But, Babe—"

Velma turned to Milty and Diane. "Thank you for waiting for me."

Milty nodded. "We should probably—" he pointed down the path.

Velma agreed. "It's coming. I just barely made it out of the bathroom." Her eyes started to well up again and she fought the tears back, swallowing any further explanation or detail. "Let's just go."

Milty jogged down the trail and the others followed. He approached Kyle, who was still standing by himself. His mouth formed a single pale line across his face and his eyes flitted this way and that. Milty grabbed him as they went by because it didn't seem immediately clear that Kyle would follow. "Come on, Kyle. It's—"

"Here." Kyle was looking straight up. Above the short forest canopy. Stars should have speckled the clear sky, but something instead cast an inky blot over the picture. An invisible force agitated one of the tallest trees and a large limb crashed to the ground in the vicinity. For a brief instant, a terrible smile began to spread on Kyle's face but disappeared the moment Milty called his name

"Kyle!" he said, rescuing his friend from whatever dreamlike state he seemed to be fading in and out of. "Go! Fast!"

And Milty ran. Everyone else, Kyle included, followed closely on his heels.

Diane had somehow ended up in the rear of their party and called up to the front. "Milty! Where are we—?"

Again, an unseen enemy clipped a couple of trees in the dark, and bits of bark and leaves rained down onto their heads.

Milty shouted back to her, no longer caring if they drew attention to themselves. "Just through here!" he said. "This path'll drop us right behind Bay Video! It's not far! We're almost there!"

And then, as if they weren't already motivated enough to run for their lives, a croupy voice—belched down to them on shredded, infected vocal cords—delivered a single word that would've, under normal circumstances, stopped any of them in their tracks. But the evil of that night was no longer fresh and their brains were gradually becoming numb to the accelerating danger and menace.

"*Want*," it seethed from a dreadfully small distance above their heads.

They all barreled onward. And just as Milty thought he could make out, beyond the trees, the faint yellow light on the back "Employees Only" entrance of Bay Video, he granted himself a moment to wonder.

Want? Do you want us or—

They burst through the woods and Milty spun his torso to make sure everyone was with him. Their expressions told him they were all frightened. None of their faces suggested otherwise.

—or did one of us want you?

CHAPTER TWENTY-FOUR

MILTY BURKITTS PLAY ▷

Bay Video

THE DOOR WAS LOCKED and Milty tried to kick it open.

Yeah, good luck with that, Jean-Claude Van Damme.

Diane joined him and together they rammed their shoulders into the entrance at the back of the building.

This isn't going to work.

The treetops a short distance behind them began to stir with more vigor. A crackling of branches announced their pursuer's imminent advent. There wasn't anywhere left to go, and so they could only keep wailing away at the door. After the shop was a parking lot and then the ocean.

Nowhere to run.

Velma whimpered, and Milty dared to peek over his shoulder. Immediately, he saw the encroaching malevolence that'd caused her to cry.

It's here.

The demon was in the process of descending from where it'd torn through the last of its wooded camouflage. A dark cloak rippled and flapped around the sea devil in a hellish, tenebrous aura. It's cowl billowed, exposing more of the Buoygeist's rotting features and the permanent smirk it directed at its hapless prey.

How is this real?

Rex and Velma ran to join them at the door. It cracked a bit under the weight of the four of them, but still wouldn't budge.

The Buoygeist, hovering mere inches from the smooth pavement, began to move closer.

"Kyle!" Milty shouted toward the one member of their group still standing and watching their assailant's approach. "What're you doing? Get over here! We need you!"

Kyle didn't move. He was fully turned around, his back to his friends. Frozen in place or intentionally waiting, Milty couldn't tell.

"Kyle!"

Diane pulled Milty back to the door. "We have to do this without him. On the count of three, let's hit it at the same time. Ready? One...two...three!"

The door shuddered but still didn't open.

The demon inched closer. Milty could hear the sound of its fluttering, dead garment.

"Again," Diane was in control now. "Give it everything you've got. One...two...three!"

And, once more, the doorway held fast.

Milty wheezed. "What now...what're we going to—?"

A light flicked on inside the shop.

Diane saw it at the same time. "Milty, someone's—"

He was already pounding on the door. "Hey! *Hey*! Let us in! Please, hurry!"

There was movement inside. Someone peeking out from behind a blind.

"Hey!" Diane chimed in. "Help us! Please, this thing is going to—"

Not further away than the length of a few parked cars, the spirit unfurled a long sinewy forearm. A barnacle-covered fist squeezed tightly to the shaft of the harpoon, still covered in the blood of its last victims.

And then the door cracked open. A voice, confident yet annoyed, called out. "Who's there?"

Milty put his face to the crack in the door. "Surge! Oh my God, please open the door. Take the chain off. We—" he turned and looked over his shoulder. Kyle was still standing in place, calmly waiting to greet the evil. "We are going to DIE. Open the goddamned door!"

Surge grumbled, clearly still not having seen what was behind them. "Alright, Son. Hold on just a damn second. Lemme get this thing—"

"Surge!" Diane screamed. "Please, hurry!"

The door swung open and they all toppled inside.

All except Kyle.

Oh, shit, Kyle!

And, as the four of them scrambled in, Surge finally got a good look at the tableau behind Bay Video. The creature's arms were stretched completely out to its sides. Kyle was stuck in place and his hair had begun to dance in the swirling winds that seemed to emanate from the monster. Surge's eyes widened.

"I'll be damned."

Faster than Milty had ever seen the man move, he leapt out into the night, wrapped both of his massive biceps around Kyle, and hefted him into the air. And then, without taking his eyes from the creature, he backed deliberately toward the door, dragging Kyle safely inside with him.

Milty slammed the door shut, bolted it, and put the chain back into place.

As if that's going to do anything.

For a moment, everyone lay collapsed on the floor of the store, panting. A few VHS tapes had been knocked from their perches, and the sticker vending machine had fallen face down, shattering bits of glass everywhere.

"Mother*fucker*," Surge said, surveying the damage.

A dark cloud moved past the windows in the back of the shop, and a sporadic screeching sound—the endblade of the harpoon dragging on the glass windows—accompanied it around to the front. When it arrived near the main entrance, the shadow paused for a second and then continued back around to the rear again.

"What's it doing?" Milty asked.

Velma stood up, tracking the thing as it started another loop around. "It doesn't make any sense. At the Drive-In, it just busted into the bathroom like the Big Bad Wolf blowing over the pig's house of sticks. Is it just messing with us?"

Surge rose to his full height. "He ain't comin' in here."

All eyes turned to him. They were haggard, exhausted, but something in the way he offered that last bit of assurance—the conviction and surety with which the shop owner made the declaration—perked them all up.

"Uh, Surge?" Milty stood up. "This thing can do whatever it wants. People have died tonight. Many, *many* people. This thing...it's the—"

"Buoygeist," Surge finished for him. "Yeah, that's him, alright. No doubt. Known him the second I saw him. We're...*old friends.*"

Surge?

No one spoke. Milty didn't know what to say or ask—what his boss was confessing didn't make any sense.

Surge took off his red bandana and dabbed his forehead before returning it. "Oh, you can all go ahead and shut your mouths before any flies get in there. Wish I had a mirror on me so you could see yourselves, *shit.*" He pointed at the darkness continuing its lap around the building. "But believe me when I say, you're safe in here. Bay Video. *My place.* At least," he scratched at the white stumble on his chin. "At least I think you are." When no one responded or reacted in any way at all, he bit his lip, clearly considering how much he wanted to say. "Ah, shit. Kids these days need you to spell every last thing out for 'em. Still don't believe me, huh? Well, listen closely and I'll tell you something. This sonofabitch knows me, *understand?* And he hasn't forgotten what I did to him the last time he showed his ugly ass face around here."

Everyone sat in stunned silence. After a moment, Surge began pulling them each, one at a time, to their feet. "Come on," he said. "Follow me."

CHAPTER TWENTY-FIVE

SURGE GARCIA

PLAY ▷

Bay Video (In The Basement)

"I HAVE SO MANY questions."

Surge laughed and pointed at a wool-blanketed cot on the opposite side of the small enclosure. Milty was the only one of his group still standing, hands on hips, like he was their spokesman. "Son, I like you—a helluva lot, actually—but would you please sit your ass down and stop acting like you're some union rep? Je-sus H."

Milty did do what he was told, and moved to the cot with the others, but didn't stop talking. "What is all this? A basement? Since when did Bay Video have a basement? And, also, why are you even here? The store closed hours ago. Shouldn't you be home in bed?"

Focus, Kid. Let's stay on target here. Stick to what's important.

Surge folded his massive arms and leaned himself against an old metal desk. "Am I under arrest? All these questions. I haven't been interrogated like this since I got back from 'Nam and decided to move myself down Cape. The looks and sourpusses they bestowed upon me when I finally submitted the application for my business license. You woulda thought all these beachfront property owners had never seen a black man before." He looked up and Milty still had an eyebrow raised. "Oh, fine. You want answers? *Fine.* Since I opened the place. My basement, that is. That's how long Bay Video has had a basement. And tonight? Well, tonight I ended up working late—on account of one lucky asshole whose shift I agreed to cover—and decided to just crash here." He smirked. "And good thing too."

The five kids were all crammed on the cot. Velma's face was in Rex's lap, and he was running his bronzed fingers through her blood-streaked hair. Diane's head rested on Milty's shoulder, and Kyle's eyes were fixated on their surroundings.

"This is no ordinary basement," Kyle mumbled to himself, but loud enough for everyone else to hear. "What is all of this?"

The walls were painted lime green, but only small peeks of the color were visible as almost every inch of the space was covered in newspaper clippings. There was a shelf of canned goods and other non-perishables. And behind Surge's head, over the desk, was a large metal weapon of some kind. It looked to be a type of firearm or cannon and was connected to a backpack with two cylinders, which hung on another hook beside it.

"What? All this?" Surge made a circular motion with his finger. "Well, this is my 'break glass in case of emergency' room."

Rex rolled his eyes. "Looks like a bomb shelter to me."

Surge looked him directly in the face and Rex immediately turned his gaze to the floor. "And who the hell are you?"

Velma spoke but didn't open her eyes or lift her head. "He's my boyfriend."

Surge growled. "Well, you tell your boyfriend that this is no bomb shelter. I'm done being afraid of bombs. Had to talk myself outta being afraid of bombs a long, long time ago. Otherwise, I'd have never slept again. Those things still live somewhere, deep in the darkest pits of my mind, but I prefer to wall 'em off. There's other stuff that needs my attention. Plenty of other things—including the one outside—that I have to worry about."

Kyle stood up then and walked to a side of the room that was particularly layered in stories cut out from the local paper. "These are all local disappearances. Unsolved. Unexplained killings. You've been tracking it—or, uh—*studying* it?"

Surge walked up and stood beside him. "Someone's got to. They—the local tourism board—they want this all to disappear.

And, in a way, it's pretty easy for 'em to disregard a lot of this because there are never any witnesses. A night jogger found dead at the marina. A kayaker discovered floating in the creek. Some poor sucker goes for a skinny dip and the body's never located. There's answers for all of that, right? More palatable answers. Answers that won't scare away the lobster roll-ers and the whale watchers and the summer renters. Anything to keep the money flowing in and the chamber of commerce happy."

Milty cleared his throat, and Surge couldn't help but smile. He liked the kid. In the seven years since the shop had opened, Milty'd worked with him for at least five. He was dependable and, even more importantly, a *good* soul. And he cared about Bay Video almost as much as Surge did himself.

Though, I wouldn't mind taking a pair of my shears to the side of his head—kid's red mop is outta control—but that's something for another day.

Milty coughed again, waiting for his boss to acknowledge him. Surge obliged. "You want something?"

Milty, his head tilted—perhaps truly seeing Surge for the first time—spoke slowly, as if he were carefully choosing his words. "So, um...why...*you*? I mean, uh—you said someone's got to—study it, er—keep tabs on it, I guess. Why *you*, though?"

Screeeeeeeeeeeeeeeeeeech.

The sound came from upstairs. The thing was still out there. Still waiting. Surge walked to the foot of the staircase and held his breath, listening to see if he'd been wrong in ushering them all down into that space without an emergency exit. When he didn't hear anything more alarming, he returned to Milty's question. "Why me, you ask?" Surge reached into the desk drawer and pulled out a box of cigars. He took one for himself and lit it with a lighter that seemed to appear out of thin air. He did *not* offer any to the rest of them.

Puffing out a cloud of smoke, his eyes squinted a bit as he considered the question that'd been posed to him. "Sometimes I ask myself the very same thing. Why *me*? Why Surge Garcia? A video store owner just tryin' to mind his own business and live his quiet, damn life? But, I know why. You see, the truth is," he took a long drag of his cigar, held it in his mouth savoring it, and then expelled the toxic cloud out and over their heads. "The truth is...I've *survived*," he nodded as if, in that moment, he was just coming to realize it himself. "I've survived. See, years ago, I was there when a fool friend of mine did what we both knew he shouldn't do. Got to the marina too late to save him, but with enough time to bear witness to the obscenity. I was there when that demon came for him. I *saw* it all and it saw *me*. He got 'ol Jerry that day. But he didn't get Surge. I lived to see another one."

Diane sat up. "But I thought—"

"You thought, *what?*" Surge stopped her. "That no one ever survived?" His deep belly laugh echoed around the green walls of the small room. "That'd be convenient storytelling, eh? But, it's true. I came face to face with that thing and I *lived*. I have no way of knowing if I'm the only one for certain—who would believe this story if anyone were to tell it? Folks around town were already so eager to ship my ass back over the bridge, that woulda been all they needed to have me rounded up and driven off to some funny farm. Nossir. Nuh uh. I've lived enough life to know that would've gotten me nowhere—would've only caused me more headaches." He pointed at the walls of clippings. "Figured I'd, instead, keep tabs on it and—go from there."

Kyle was still pacing the room, his eyes glossed over. "But, *how?*"

Surge smiled. "How'd I live? How am I standing here, on this very night, to tell the tale? Well—and this is important; this is why you came to the right place this evening—when he came for me on that night, only a few years before this shop opened up its doors in fact, I decided to fight back. And, in fighting back, realized it can be hurt." His grin grew even wider, exposing two rows of gleaming white teeth. "And so, I hurt him."

Diane was leaning fully forward, her hat slightly askew—her hair displaced and wild on either side of it. "*How?*"

Screeeeeeeeeeeeeeech.

Surge walked to the staircase again and looked up. "Fire. Heat. Those many years ago, all I had was a gasoline-drenched tiki torch. But even that bit of *MacGyver* action did the trick." He pointed a thumb at the wall behind him. "Still, I decided I'd upgrade, in the event it ever came back looking for me." He reached up and patted the weapon on its side, like a prize pony. "It's a flamethrower. Military grade. Best one video store money can buy. I call her Wanda, after my old flame... *Wanda*. She still gets me all hot and bothered."

Milty raised his hand, unnecessarily. "Uh, so that's it? Just...*fire*?"

Surge nodded. "Yep. That's it." He could see, based on the number of hoisted eyebrows, that not all of them were buying what he was selling. "You have to remember, this thing is from the sea. It's made, at least in large part, of water. And heat and water, last I checked, don't exactly mix." Surge took another puff of his cigar. "In any case, he knows that I know his little secret. He knows I'm ready for his undead ass."

Diane clapped her hands together, excitedly. "And *that's* why he won't come in here."

Surge lifted his shoulders and then brought them back down. "Best I can tell. But it's hard to know for certain. That thing won't be satiated until all of you—every last one of you who were there beside that blighted buoy—are dead. Or the sun comes up. Whichever happens first."

CHAPTER TWENTY-SIX

MILTY BURKITTS

PLAY ▷

Bay Video (Back Upstairs)

AT FIRST, HE DIDN'T see it.

Is it gone?

Milty carefully poked his head out from behind Surge's much larger frame. They were both standing at the top of the staircase. Surge had donned the flamethrower, and the two canisters were cold to the touch as Milty brushed up against them. After nearly an hour of the group all holed up downstairs, the two had agreed on a reconnaissance mission to sneak back into the store to see if the spirit had departed. Surge had also promised to return with a few buckets of popcorn to tide them all over a bit longer.

"See anything?" Diane called up to them from the basement.

Milty inched forward following in Surge's deliberate footsteps. The back of the older man's neck was slick, beading a river of sweat, and Milty took note of how powerful and unyielding the shop owner seemed. Milty wasn't sure of Surge's exact age—*fiftyish?*—but he did know that he was glad the man was taking the lead.

Finally, someone else is in charge.

Milty craned his own neck. He could see out the back of the store, in the direction they'd traveled from earlier that evening. There was very little light that way, but he didn't notice anything out of sorts. "I don't see anything—" he gulped down what he'd been about to say. As his head swung to the front of the store, it finally moved into his line of sight. Hovering just in front of the largest of the shop windows—the one next to the main entrance, where Surge typically hung signage advertising the newest arrivals and ongoing deals—was the cursed villain. It wasn't moving, fixed in position, and its cloak hung in torn, soiled shreds like infernal tentacles. Its head, still mostly hidden beneath a withered cowl, was cocked unnaturally to the side. And—

It's staring in at us.

It was staring in at them.

"Hold on," Surge cautioned, the nozzle of his weapon raised. "He's watching."

Milty nodded, though Surge couldn't see him.

"W-what do we do then?"

Surge gestured behind himself. "Downstairs. Not safe to be up here yet."

Just as Milty's foot hit the top stair again and it began to creak, the store was suddenly illuminated by a blue, flashing light. They both lurched to a stop.

"Sonofabitch," Surge grumbled.

"What is it?"

Surge took a step back into the store. "What does it look like? It's the law. Getting in the way. Surprise, surprise."

Milty heard the contempt in the man's voice.

And then he heard a police car door slam closed.

"Shit. This is bad," Surge's grip on the flamethrower tightened. "Here we go."

Everything was so quiet that even the crunching of the police officer's standard-issue footwear was audible.

Milty winced, bracing himself for what he feared was about to happen.

No, no, no, no.

And then—then all hell broke loose.

"Police! Let me see your hands!"

"Oh, you have *got* to be kidding."

Milty stepped closer to Surge. "Can you see anything?"

"I see a police officer 'bout to get herself killed, that's what I see."

A few more footsteps and the gravel underneath them being disturbed. Again, the officer called out. "Hey! I said show me your hands!"

The Buoygeist obliged. Its arms began to languidly unpack themselves from where they'd been concealed. The harpoon flashed brilliantly under the blue lights.

Run lady, just run.

Milty heard her choke on her own astonishment and then immediately start firing.

"No!" Surge called out. "Goddammit."

From down below, Diane called up again. "What is that?" She sounded like she was at least halfway up the staircase. "What's that noise? It sounds like—"

"Stay down there!" Milty called. "It's not safe, please—"

And just as Diane appeared behind him out of the darkness, the demon spun to face the police offer.

"Oh my God!" the woman screamed.

The harpoon twirled. Two more shots were fired, one piercing the storefront window. Surge gestured toward the floor. "Get your asses down!"

But his warning was not in time for the two of them to avoid seeing what happened next. The Buoygeist, unimpeded by the officer's pistol, lifted itself higher into the night sky before descending on the woman like a Great Blue Heron stabbing at an Atlantic mackerel. Its harpoon pierced her directly through the stomach, and the creature turned back toward the store, displaying his bleeding trophy. The cop's gun fell from her hands, but she was dead by the time it hit the ground. A final tremor ran through her body before the demon twirled the carcass around a couple of times for show.

It's taunting us.

"No!" Surge cried out again. "No more." He turned and winked at Milty. "I'm so sick of this asshole."

"Wait, *Surge*—"

But it was too late. He wasn't to be stopped. Surge stormed toward the exit.

"Surge!" Milty called to him, though the man was already kicking the door open.

"Alright, ya bastahd! Time to die!"

Milty wasn't sure whose "time" he meant. He started to move in the same direction, just as Surge disappeared outside, but Diane grabbed him.

"Stop! Are you insane?"

Milty pointed toward the door. He could hear the roar of the flamethrower and Surge's R-rated diatribe. "I need to help him."

Diane shook her head. "No. No, you definitely do not." She squeezed his elbow, and he allowed himself to breathe. "We're getting the others and then—" she pointed out the back door. "And then we're getting the hell outta here."

The Parking Lot

VELMA WAS THE LAST out of the building. She'd been the only one who thought it a better idea to stay put, but no one else seemed to agree. The others, Rex included, had left her pleading for them to come back, but eventually she—quite begrudgingly—followed. When she stepped outside, Milty was waving to get her attention, not wanting to shout or alert the creature to their escape. The lone light at the back entrance of the shop only gave so much illumination, so he had to really flop around for her to see him.

Velma sprinted over. "I can't believe you guys just left me. *Again.*"

Milty put a finger to his lips, his eyes wide and frantic, and pointed toward the front of the store. He whispered. "It's still over there. Listen."

Surge's voice traveled to their ears. Much of what he said was hard to make out—a great deal of grunting interspersed between the roar of the flame thrower and a few sprinkled-on curses for good measure. "Watcha gonna do?" they heard his booming voice jab at the thing. "Not so tough now, huh?"

Milty took a few steps in the direction of the skirmish, but Diane quickly leapt out in front of him. Velma noted how quickly Milty stopped when Diane touched him.

Hmm, she thought. *That's new.*

"We need to help him," Milty argued.

"No," Diane said. "He—what's he's doing—it's giving us an opening. A chance to escape. *We need to take it.*"

Milty tried to push past her, but Velma chimed in. "You know she's right, Milty." He stopped but wouldn't look at her. "We gotta get outta here. While we still can. Otherwise, what was the point of us leaving the basement? Once that thing's finished with Surge—"

Milty snarled at her, over his shoulder. "Don't say that. He's my friend—"

"Yeah, and so are *we*." Velma sighed and then tried a softer tone. "Look, if we don't start moving, we're next. It's as simple as that. And I'm *freaking* out. We *were* safe, and now—we're *not*. We're just standing out here in the open. Waiting for that thing to come and get us. And it will. Soon."

Not gonna sugarcoat it.

Milty nodded and, at almost the same moment, Surge cried out. "Auuugh, you sonofa—" One instant the shop owner was taunting the demon, and, in the next, his jeers quickly metamorphosized into groans that suggested sudden inflicted pain. Agony.

He's hurt.

"Surge!"

Diane threw her hand around Milty's mouth and Velma wrapped her arms around him. "Help me, Rex, goddammit."

Before Rex could even touch him, Milty pushed them all away. "I'm fine, I'm *fine*." He looked in the direction of Surge's continued wailing, obviously not wanting to leave but understanding they had no other reasonable option. "So, what do we do now then?"

Velma knew the answer, but she waited for someone else to suggest something.

Say it.

No one spoke up. Their eyes all flitted from one face to the other.

How did I figure this out before anyone else?

Surge's thrower gave a feeble, final-sounding rumble. One last belch before—

Tell them!

"I—"

Milty and Diane were whispering, their heads together, still not being forthcoming with any sort of solution. Kyle was sitting on the ground, long past being completely checked out. And Rex just shrugged. Nobody had heard Velma start to speak, at least partly because no one expected her to.

"Guys—" she tried again.

Everyone ignored her. No one ever looked to her for answers, though she often had them.

"Hey!" she hissed loud enough to draw their stares. They all blinked at her. Finally having everyone's attention, she spit it out.

The answer.

"Fire," she said. "That's it. That's the answer."

Rex flapped the bottom of his shirt as if airing himself out. "What answer, Babe? What're you—?"

"Shut up, Rex," she snapped, barely looking at him. Instead, she addressed the other three. "Fire. Remember? I mean—Surge said that's what would *hurt it.*"

Milty rubbed at his eyes. "Yeah, but—Surge's got it. The flamethrower. And, by the sound of it—"

"The *bonfires*, idiot. You forgetting those? They'll still be going. Ours may be out, but you know as well as I do there are still people there. Probably will be lined all up and down the beach 'til the early morning on a Friday night." She gestured toward the ocean. "And it's Homecoming. Everyone's... *come home* to party."

Milty and Diane were already nodding. "You're right," he said, pointing his chin at the far side of the lot. "And we're close too. Just down the dunes. Bet there's still a few ragers."

Velma started jogging. "Exactly," she glanced over her shoulder but didn't slow her pace. "Well, okay, let's go. Come on!"

One by one they all followed her lead.

Nice going, Vel.

And just as they approached the Dune, she caught—out of the corner of her eye—the demon lowering itself over something else. Something wet and squirming.

Something pleading for mercy.

She spun her face away and sensed the others did too. No one said anything because there was nothing to be said. There was nothing to be done. They crested the dune, found the hurricane-tested, wooden staircase leading to the beach, and ignored the death screams that chased them toward the aphotic shores of Cape Cod Bay.

Chapter Twenty-Eight

Milty Burkitts

PLAY ▷

Another Bonfire

AT THE BOTTOM OF the staircase, there was dense smoke. Or fog. It was hard to tell which. The low-lying cloud hung over the sand and the water, and—littering the winding shoreline, as far as the eye could see—were little flickering embers. Bonfires. High school kids. Others, home for the weekend from college. Faint laughs were audible, and the occasional hoot and accompanying holler carried to their ears on the light breeze. The pile of footwear at the base of the stairs—made up almost entirely of foam flip-flops and Birkenstocks—suggested that the beach was packed, even at that early morning hour.

There was a loud crash and Milty jumped. Velma did too, by the sound of the squeak she made from a few feet behind him. But he quickly realized the noise was of no concern.

Waves. Big, big ones tonight. High tide.

Milty tried to swallow, but his throat was parched and he'd inhaled just a bit too much of some drifting campfire smoke. He coughed and Diane slapped him on the back.

"You okay?" she asked without slowing her hurried speed-walk across the sand.

Milty shook his head. "No."

She didn't press him further or inquire why. Surge's screams had stopped. Milty knew there was nothing more she needed to know. Nothing else he needed to say. He *wasn't* okay.

Surge is gone.

Milty felt his eyes start to well, and he didn't bother to wipe at them. There wasn't time.

He bought us a minute, but we need to get to one of those bonfires now.

The closest to them was decent in size. Even though it'd been burning for hours, there was still life around its perimeter. A couple of guys around his age, beers in hand, sat quietly in their beach chairs staring into the flames. They had a stack of store-bought logs in between their seats and one of them reached over and tossed on another. A few additional lifeless shapes lay sprawled, still within the warm and surprisingly far-reaching orange glow. A couple of girls curled up, asleep, under a fleece blanket. Some guy—still wearing his pizza delivery uniform—lying flat with his arms folded over his chest, his head precariously close to the lapping fingers of the Atlantic.

Right here, Milty thought as the five of them ambled over, raggedly materializing out of the darkness. Panting. *This'll do.*

One of the two still-somewhat-alert guys pushed the brim of his hat up casually with an index finger. "Hey, gang. Hey, fellas." His smile was welcoming, but his decision to refer to them all as both "gang" *and* "fellas"—and the speed at which he drawled the greeting—suggested he was well over the legal limit. Milty thought he looked familiar, though couldn't place him or remember his name. Probably someone a few years older, back home for the weekend. "Hey, there," the guy tried again. "We're almost ready to call it a night, but feel free to—"

Milty rushed to his side and collected an armful of skinny logs. "Something's coming," he interrupted, as he handed them out. "You better arm yourself with one of these."

The guy blinked. "What's coming?" His speech was a bit slurred, and the question actually came out of his mouth like, "Werrts cerrrmin'?"

Milty ignored him, shouting instructions. "Get any pieces of fabric you can find. Tear off strips of your shirts if you have to. Use a sock or two. Whatever it takes. Wrap a log and then light it." Everyone in his party immediately started following his instructions, but the guys in the chairs just stared at him. Milty pulled off his sweatshirt and tore it in half at a seam. As he wrapped his own log, he looked sideways at the two who still hadn't reacted and then glanced at the three still asleep. "Better wake your friends up."

The second bro cackled. He was quite large and occupied more than his fair share of his chair. "Yah. Good luck with that, *Guy*."

Milty shrugged. "Up to you, but any second there's gonna be something terrible coming over those dunes behind us. And fire's the only thing that'll hurt it."

The larger one flailed toward the bonfire. "Well, watcha call this?"

Milty was about to respond when his eyes happened to glance back toward the staircase. At the very top of the steps, rising over the dune, was the unrelenting, implacable creature that hunted them. The massive, greasy splotch on the horizon lifted itself toward the cosmos, blocking out the only driblet of moonlight that'd managed to breach the increasing cloud cover.

"Everyone. Get ready. *It's here.*"

And the monster descended. Slowly. A shadow slithering down the sandy slope, its only obstacles were a few blades of parched grass and a bit of liberated campfire smoke that'd drifted off too far into the night.

"Light 'em!" Diane was the first to stick her socked-wrapped log into the blaze. It caught quickly. "And then keep your back to the bonfire!"

Before the demon had crossed the small sliver of beach that the tide hadn't claimed, the group from the video store all had their torches alight. Those that'd been quietly enjoying their evening and their beers, hadn't followed suit. As the Buoygeist floated closer, the inferno cast the ghost's face in a ghastly orange hue. Milty shuddered. It reminded him of a maggot-chewed Jack-o-lantern that'd once been left for too long on his parents' front walkway.

Oh, gross.

The Jack-o-lantern smiled as it raised its weapon but stopped before it got too close. It floated far above their heads—high enough that any of them had enough space to attempt running directly underneath it—but somehow, even at that height, Milty could still *smell it*.

Oh my God.

A mixture of salt water, decay, and vomit. That's the only way he could describe what wafted into his nostrils. He, mirroring everyone else, covered his nose with a free hand.

The stench caused the larger of the two chair-ridden guys to swing his head around. "Dang. What the *fuck* is that?"

Milty didn't take his eyes off the hovering assassin. He kept the sizzling log in front of himself, his arms straightened fully out so as not to burn his own eyebrows off. "Don't," he cautioned.

The first guy struggled to stand but eventually got to his feet. "Wick-*ed!*" he lifted his beer in salute and then took a big swig. "It's the pahty-stahta!" he said, his "r's" getting dropped gratuitously in typical Massachusetts fashion.

Idiots.

Velma and Rex were just behind the two in the chairs, between them and the bonfire. Velma tried to get the attention of the drunkards. "Shhh," she pleaded. "*Sit down.*"

The second guy stood up then too, his chair knocked to the ground behind him in the process. He stumbled a few steps in the direction of the monster, pressed his can to his lips, and drained the remainder of his drink. When finished, he belched and then crumpled the empty can in his fist as if he were performing some fantastic feat of strength. "Yeaaaah, baby!" he howled and then bobbled a couple more steps forward, his feet not even lifting out of the cold sand, his eyes hanging so low with intoxication that he couldn't possibly have been able to see much.

The Buoygeist hefted his spear high.

The round man struggled to remove his shirt and then swung it around his head a few times. "Yeaaaah!" he shouted. "Badass costume, Bro! Where'd ya get it?"

The demon didn't advance, but it did tilt its head to one side, examining the man like a puppy might look with curiosity at an ant.

The other guy lumbered over. "Sir! Sir!" he called. "D'you hear m'friend? He wants to know...where'd you get it? Your costume?" He stared blankly when the thing did not offer a response. "Ok, Man. I get it. I get it. It's cool. Well, give me five!" And then he stuck out his hand.

Milty winced.

As if the menace had been waiting, its harpoon twirled through the air, released like the spring of a mouse trap, and sliced the man's arm off at the shoulder. The wound was ragged, shreds of red pulp glistening in the brilliance of the fire, and left a steady stream squirting onto the once white sand.

"Aaaaaaaauuuuuugh!" the guy cried, staring in shock at his new stump, his eyes already beginning to roll up into the back of his head. He collapsed to the ground.

Velma screamed. Kyle skittered around to the backside of the campfire, hiding out of view.

The armless man's friend tripped backward and, before he could regain his footing, the monster drifted closer—bringing itself directly over him. The man started to stammer, but, whether it was due to the crippling fear suddenly coursing through his bloodstream or all the beers he'd just consumed, couldn't get much out of his mouth that was immediately comprehensible. He put his hands up in front of his face. "N-n-no—I—ohhh—n-n-no." And then the demon speared directly through his palms and into his throat. The man sputtered, then shuddered, then sighed deeply before an aqueous burp escaped his lips and he went silent.

"Everyone, stay where you are!" Milty cried out. "Don't move!"

It was right about then that the other three—the two sleeping women and the pizza delivery guy—woke up. As their eyes fluttered open, they each immediately took note of the carnage. And of the giant, cloaked thing not too far above their heads.

Diane tried to calm them, preemptively. "Please, just stay here! Stay near the fire, don't do anything—"

But it was too late. Diane could not stop them, nor would she or anyone else risk their lives to try and prevent the three from running off into the night.

Which is exactly what happened next.

The two women, screaming, made a run for the staircase. Before either had escaped the lambent boundary and its flickering, diabolical glow, both were quickly dispatched without—it seemed—much effort or exertion on the part of the demon. Indeed, it was with a single swing of the nautical bayonet that both were taken down. One was cleaved completely across the midsection and the other slashed in the back. The two instantly crumpled to the ground and did not move again.

Stupid, stupid, stupid, stupid.

The pizza delivery guy was up to his waist in the waves before the Bouygeist noticed him. When he saw the creature flying in his direction, the man dove into the ocean and attempted a rather pathetic breaststroke. In the end, neither his swimming technique nor the waves were a deterrent. The harpoon—perhaps even more at home in the frigid, salty depths—flew out of the creature's hand and stuck firmly to the spot where the delivery guy foolishly attempted to hide himself underwater. Even with the minimal amount of orange light that dappled the waves, it was immediately clear he too was gone. The water quickly turned a dark shade of red, like someone had just tossed out a bucket of chum to some hungry sharks, and the creature flew over to easily retrieve the dart it'd thrown.

"Don't move!" Milty reminded everyone—as if they needed reminding—and the five of them kept their backs to the hearth. "Don't let him spook you! That's exactly what he wants!" The devil began to orbit the group like a seagull circling a netted school of Atlantic menhaden. Each of them had their personal incendiary held prominently in front of their faces.

"Should we take him?" Rex said, weighing whether or not they should fight back.

Even in the heat of battle, Velma could find time to roll her eyes at him. "Take him? Are you fucking nuts? Are you *high*? Did you see what he just—?"

"Shhh," Kyle whispered from somewhere behind them. From somewhere in the dark. In the shadows. "He's waiting for us. He's waiting for us to slip up, to lose focus."

Though Milty had long since ruled Kyle "out of commission" he had to agree. "Exactly. He expects us to do something foolish. Like the others." He looked at the bodies strewn about nearby. "Don't be like the others."

And then Kyle spoke up again, keeping his eyes trained on the Buoygeist as it continued to circle its prey. "By the way," he said, just loudly enough for them all to hear. "Which one of you called him?"

No one responded, and—once the awkward silence had lingered for a bit too long—Kyle asked again.

"I said, which one of you—?"

"Was it *you*, Kyle?" Velma asked, getting annoyed. "Is that what you want to tell us? As if it's some huge shocking reveal. I'm sure I'm not the only one who's been getting a super weird vibe from you tonight."

Kyle chuckled. It was the wrong time to chuckle. "It wasn't me, Vel." He laughed again, though this time with far less amusement lacing his vocal chords. "It wasn't me."

Everyone remained silent. Milty was about to suggest to Kyle exactly where he could stuff his stupid—incredibly unhelpful—line of questioning when the Buoygeist suddenly flittered away into the night. There one moment and—*flutter, flap, flutter*—gone the next. Back over the dune. Away from them. Away from the fire.

Nobody moved. They all kept their positions.

"What do we do now?" Velma asked, her voice trembling more and more as the evening progressed.

Milty gulped. It seemed like he was in charge now. As all the tired, terror-stricken faces trained in his direction suggested, Velma—and maybe everyone else—expected him to already have some sort of a plan. Expected him to tell the rest of them what to do next. He opened his mouth. "Well, I think—"

"We wait." Diane looked each of them in the eyes to make sure they were listening. "*We wait.* It's not time to lose our goddamn shit. Understand? This thing might come back, but we don't need to be doing anything other than standing here. Fire to our backs. Fire in our hands. Where it's safe."

Milty nodded, grateful for her confidence and her leadership. He gave her a thumbs up. It was a feeble show of support, but the evening had drained him of all else.

Yes, Diane, he agreed, quietly to himself. *We wait.*

CHAPTER TWENTY-NINE

SURGE GARCIA   PLAY ▷

The Parking Lot

SURGE GARCIA OPENED HIS EYES.

CHAPTER THIRTY

DIANE SHAW

PLAY ▷

Fire At Their Backs

DIANE WATCHED MILTY.

Where'd you go?

For the longest time, she'd been looking at him. Staring at him, really, but he hadn't seemed to notice.

Does he ever?

Milty was peering into the flame that burned brightly at the top of his log. Peering *through* it, perhaps. She'd wished he'd suddenly just offer up what he was thinking and begin divulging whatever was racing through his brain. What *was* he doing? Was he thinking through their next steps? Was he meditating? Was he asleep with his eyes open or otherwise completely checked out? Diane couldn't tell, but she really wanted to know.

"Hey, Milty?" she said, abruptly. The words had just fallen out, even surprising herself.

Even more unexpectedly and out of character, he coolly turned to her and smiled. "Hey, Diane."

She screwed her mouth up to one side of her face, trying to get a read on him. "You, uh, doing okay?"

His grin, suddenly uninhibited, hadn't yet dissipated. He ran his tongue over his teeth casually and shrugged. "Yeah. I mean, *no*, not at all. But, *yeah*. Sure."

They were all sitting on the sand at this point, still surrounding the fire with their torches—which they'd each stuck in the ground between their legs. It'd been a good twenty minutes at least since the demon had made its unforeseen, confounding exit and they had no way of knowing when or if it'd make an equally unforeseen, confounding return. Aside from quite literally resting on their laurels, no one had done *anything*—or made any attempt to run or suggest an alternative to sitting in place and waiting things out. Rex was balancing his chin on his knees, and Velma shockingly—or perhaps not so—was *not* leaning her head on his shoulder. In fact, she'd actually increased the distance between herself and her boyfriend, a gap that was perhaps an illustration of the growing divide in their relationship. Kyle was still by himself on the opposite side of the campfire, staring out into the sea. Now and again, Diane thought she heard him mumbling to himself. Once he'd even laughed out loud, which might have been the most disquieting sound she'd heard that entire evening. The flames of the pyre had died down significantly, and, as no one in the group had any interest in separating themselves and walking to the pile of logs for more fuel, it would undoubtedly continue to do so.

"Yeah?" she said, still unsure how to take Milty's atypical smile. "Well, that's good. I'm—I'm—"

Milty was still turned toward her. *Looking* at her. It was something new and Diane liked it.

"We're all pretty effed up right now. It's okay."

"Yeah," she said, not disagreeing. "But, it's not just...well, *that*. I guess I—I feel responsible for this. For us being here. For, well, *everything*." Milty blinked, and she continued. "Tonight probably wouldn't have happened like this if not for me."

Milty, still fully focused on her, shook his head. "That's insane, Diane. How could you put any of this on yourself?"

She shrugged. "You didn't want to come tonight, remember?"

Milty lifted one eyebrow. "So?"

"So," Diane sighed. "So, if I hadn't dragged you here—you know, *convinced* you to come, well...well, you'd be home in bed right now. So would I. And no one would've been there to feed Rex's ridiculous need to *see* that thing. The buoy. Velma certainly wasn't gonna take him herself."

Milty held up a hand. He looked to see if Velma or Rex were listening, but the pops and crackles in the fire seemed loud enough to hide their conversation—loud enough for the both of them to continue without speaking any more softly. No one else seemed to stir or react at all to what Diane had said. "Well, lemme just stop you right there. If anything, it was *my* bravado and my—*whatever*—my need to not play the coward tonight. If anything, *that* was what got us all into this mess. You just wanted to hang out with me. Nothing inherently wrong with that."

"Milty—"

"No. It's true. If I'd just told Rex to go screw—" he reacted to the corner of her mouth turning up in a smirk. "What? I say something—"

Kiss him.

Diane froze.

What, like...now?

The lines on Milty's forehead were increasing in size and number. He was struggling to read her mind.

Yes.

"Diane...you still with me?"

No. This isn't some dumb movie. In real life, people don't kiss when everyone around them is being hunted and slaughtered by a demon with a harpoon.

She nodded—as if finally convincing herself—and sighed, disappointed but also relieved with her decision.

"Oh, um," she tried to recover. "Yeah, you're right. Guess we both share some of the blame for tonight. Thanks for saying so."

Milty finally released her from his gaze and turned his focus back to his torch. "I'd prefer if neither of us took *ownership* of this madness. This—this could not have been predicted."

Diane was about to open her mouth, about to thank him and simultaneously confess her decade-long crush on him, when the skies suddenly opened up.

It started to rain.

"Oh, no," she said.

Immediately, the fire—at their backs and in their hands—began to sizzle. Smoke billowed and, what started as a light rain—within seconds—turned into a heavy downpour.

Do something. Before—

Diane jumped to her feet. Without thinking, she started shouting commands. "To The Fry Fry. Back up the stairs. We have to hurry. Now! Let's go!"

And the others followed. Wordlessly they ran as she ran. Clutching their flames, hoping to get under cover before their last line of defense was extinguished.

Diane saw Milty beside her, keeping pace. Stride for stride. She caught a sob in her throat and forced it down before it could escape her mouth.

Before our lives are extinguished.

CHAPTER THIRTY-ONE

MILTY BURKITTS

PLAY ▷

The Fry Fry

MILTY'S TORCH WAS ALREADY snuffed by the time they reached The Fry Fry.

Shit.

Diane, Velma, and Rex still had live flames when they arrived at the closed-for-the-night food shack. Kyle's had also gone out, doused by the sudden rain shower. The five of them crowded, shoulder to shoulder, under the awning—making sure to keep the remaining torches lowered so as not to set the entire building on fire. Though a single, fixed lightbulb—centered on the underside of the overhang—provided some added illumination, it also cast a sickly, yellow glow to their already sweat and soot-stained faces. Each of them looked depleted, disoriented, and scared.

"We all here?" Of course, Milty could see that everyone *was*, but his anxiety compelled him to ask just the same. No one answered. All eyes peered into the darkness, anticipating what wet horror might suddenly appear out of the downpour. Milty dragged a forearm across his face, swiping at the tributaries that beaded from his soggy curls, and shivered. He held his sizzling torch like a cudgel.

I know you're out there.

The rain was steady and didn't appear to be letting up. Diane—shifting her sopping wet bangs from one side of her face to the other—pointed at his still-smoking log. "Gimme. We need to relight that. And yours, Kyle. Before it—"

Screeeeeeeeeeeech.

Everyone stood motionless. The sound came from over their heads. Something was dragging along the aluminum roof of the seasonal burger joint.

There we go. Took no time at all.

Milty put his index finger to his lips, but the others didn't need any directive to remain quiet. No one was going to say a damned thing. All ears were cocked to the discordant commotion from above. They waited, listening for it to come again.

Screeeeeeeeeeeech. The same sound.

A blast of saturated wind hit them then, and another torch went out. This time it was Rex's. He cursed under his breath. Only two remained alight, both of which were starting to dim.

Screeeeeeeeeeeeeech.

Milty waved at everyone to get their attention. He had to use his trucker cap to swat Kyle on the back because he was distracted, looking off into the darkness again. Once all of their eyes—Kyle's included—were locked onto his, Milty took a necessary risk and whispered, "It's taunting us. Just stay still—"

"But our torches," Velma hissed. "Mine and Diane's are almost out too. Then what?"

Milty didn't know. He didn't have an answer. But, in reality, it didn't matter. Even if the solution to their predicament had been obvious, there wouldn't have been time for him to offer a response.

The Buogeist appeared. Directly in front of the building. One moment it wasn't there, and then the next was slowly lowering itself so that it hovered only just outside the reach of The Fry Fry's faint light. Its depraved smile was even wider—somehow even more craven and revolting—than it'd been before. Again, it tilted its neck to examine them as they cowered behind their last two, quickly disappearing flames. An eel, black and mucilaginous, escaped from one of its eye holes and was consumed by the darkness inside the demon's cowl.

Velma gagged and Rex tried to put an arm around her. She brushed him away.

Milty took a step forward and Diane, protecting him with her torch, stepped up beside him. He nodded to her and she nodded back.

"Hey!" he shouted over the pounding of the torrential rain. The deluge was so loud he had no way of knowing if the thing could hear him.

Hell, I don't know if it even has ears.

He took another step, all the while making sure to not leave the safety of The Fry Fry's yellow awning. "I said, hey! You!" he gulped, squinting through the raindrops, summoning every last bit of courage in his body. "Hey, you—you—uh—you, bastard! Yeah, that's right, Asshole. I'm talking to you! Can you hear me? What do you want from us?" Out of the corner of his eye, he thought he could feel warmth and encouragement radiating off of a trembling smile from Diane.

There was a long pause and, for an instant, the only audible sound was the rain hitting the aluminum roof and pouring off the gutter-less structure in sheets. The demon hung there, suspended over the parking lot in front of The Fry Fry, as a river wept from the folds of its decomposing frock and formed a puddle beneath it. Milty opened his mouth to repeat himself but stopped when he heard the thing begin to laugh. It was incredibly low, at first—emanating from somewhere deep, somewhere bathed in alluvium and layers of rot and malodorous muck. The sound rose like a noxious, rancid bubble and popped over their heads loud enough to be heard clearly through the rain.

"Deathhhhhhhhhh," it rasped. "Only deathhhhhhhhhhh."

Behind Milty and Diane, Velma squealed. "It's out. My torch is out."

Diane stepped in front of Milty—

No.

—her flame being the sole survivor.

"Stay behind me," she instructed.

No, Diane. Stop.

"Milty!" She grabbed him and pushed him back with the others.

For some reason, he couldn't speak. Words failed. He could only watch Diane face the ghost, with her torch just barely hanging on.

And the wind whipped.

Diane.

And the rain beat down over their heads.

Diane!

And the Buoygeist patiently waited.

"Diane!"

But Milty's scream came too late. The light of Diane's torch had gone out.

Poof.

The demon saw and quickly straightened its neck. Milty swore he could hear the cracking of its monolithic vertebrae.

"Everybody, run!"

The Buoygeist readied its weapon and they all scattered—like mindless sand fleas—into the cold, austere dunes.

Chapter Thirty-Two

Diane Shaw

PLAY ▷

The Dunes

SAND. DIANE'S EYES, NOSE, and mouth were almost completely submerged in it. She was lying face-down, having tumbled a considerable distance over the first dune she'd come across. The drop-off had been far steeper than she'd predicted, and the lack of any sort of illumination made the fall all the more startling to her. Velma and Kyle had followed her journey over the edge and lay on either side of her—she could feel their bodies brushing up against hers—and she wondered if their faces were sunk into the gritty powder too. Diane hadn't seen where Milty or Rex had ended up.

Don't move.

She couldn't hear anything besides the pattering of the persistent rain and the crackling of the long-dried grasses as the winds bent and hammered them. The sand was wet and cold, and the strong perfume of the beach crept directly into her nostrils. Deciding to disregard her own warning to stay still, Diane lifted her head, daring to take a peek at their surroundings.

Kyle was looking right at her.

Kyle?

He held a finger to his lips and then pointed upward. Over their heads. Diane let her eyes follow the direction he was gesturing.

Ho-ly—

Floating, directly over the three of them, was the Buoygeist. Diane couldn't see its face or where its attention was directed, but its position and proximity suggested the possibility that it didn't see them—perhaps they were shielded from view by the thing's massive girth and the flapping folds of its threadbare robe.

Is it possible we are camouflaged? Can it not see us?

Kyle was still staring at her. Waiting for Diane to look at him again. "I don't think it knows we're here," he mouthed, silently. "I don't think it—"

Thhhwwwwap.

Kyle was wrenched up into the night by his feet, barely able to grab a handful of sand before he departed.

Velma screamed.

Diane screamed.

They both watched as Kyle was lifted higher and higher into the sky. He was writhing—fighting back. They could see that much. But, whether or not he was pleading for mercy, they couldn't tell. The height at which the demon had already carried him made it impossible for them to hear anything beyond the wind and rain as it whipped across and pulverized the exposed hummock.

CHAPTER THIRTY-THREE

KYLE CROWELL

Above It All

WITH HIS FREE LEG, Kyle continued to kick. The ground beneath him was getting further away by the second, and he could no longer even locate Diane or Velma. The wind and rain hit him in the face at such a high velocity that he could only open his eyelids for brief seconds at a time, blinking the water out just as his vision became blurred again. Looking up his dangling torso at the gray-skinned, barnacle-covered hand wrapped around his ankle, Kyle caught a whiff of the wraith's gaminess. It smelled like a beached pilot whale left out to rot in the sun and pummeling tides for weeks. He would've wretched but had already voided the contents of his stomach once since being lifted into the night. The air around Kyle was getting even heavier with moisture, and he could feel cool clouds embrace him as the earth was completely hidden from his view.

This is it, you know it is.

He tried to reach out with a hand, but—far from having any acrobatic talent whatsoever—knew immediately that effort was going nowhere.

It's too late.

He couldn't tell if they were even still rising. Everything was completely dark, and it was nearly impossible to orient himself or gauge how high up they were. He kicked out again with his foot, though quickly realized he didn't even know what he wanted to happen. If he fell from that height, it didn't matter how pillowy the dunes were or if he somehow managed to land in the water. He'd never stand a chance.

But you knew this was going to happen, right?

Kyle'd been in a stupor ever since he'd first seen the thing eviscerating Dale. A voice in his head had whispered a promise to him, right then—a promise that he'd been unable to ignore. He'd believed it, and the rest of the evening had been fuzzy, hard to focus on, like he was trying to watch the grim events unfold through streaking windshield wipers or a scrambled cable channel. The voice, whether it'd been his own or one projected from a more omniscient source, replayed its guarantee over and over again. He hadn't been able to block it out.

You will never see another morning, it'd said. *Your blood will rain from the sky.*

Kyle choked. It was getting harder to breathe. The air was thinning and water continued to disappear up his nose and into his gasping mouth.

You will never see another morning. Your blood will rain from the sky.

Kyle stopped kicking his leg. He ceased his wriggling and his writhing. Allowing his body to go limp, he let his lungs fill—as best as he could—with the sweet aroma of the sea. Kyle wanted it to be a lasting sensation, one he might carry with him wherever he went next.

You will never see another morning. Your blood will rain from the sky.

He closed his eyes—

You will never see another morning. Your blood will rain from the sky.

—sensed the grip on his leg clench tighter—

You will never see another morning. Your blood will rain from the sky.

—and braced himself—

You will never see another morning. Your blood will rain from the sky.

—for the end.

Warmth spread across Kyle's midsection. Right over his navel. It was a brief, searing, agony. And, as he tumbled away—just before his eyesight completely faded into a black, anesthetized, void—he caught one final glimpse of his tormentor still holding tightly to a pair of denim-covered legs. Redness, like fruit punch, poured out into the gloom—but quickly lost its potency as the storm clouds watered it down with their own special recipe.

Kyle's body relaxed. Though he did depart with the brininess of the Atlantic blasting by him, he also was left with one nagging voice.

You will never see another morning. Your blood will rain from the sky.

And he didn't.

And it did.

CHAPTER THIRTY-FOUR

MILTY BURKITTS PLAY ▷

On The Stairs

THE STAIRCASE SHUDDERED AND groaned as a particularly strong gust barreled into it. Milty braced himself, his back flat to the balusters and the handrail, but his flip-flopped feet slipped on the sand-swept platform and he fell hard onto his ass. Rex was squatting on the opposite side of the same platform, about halfway between the parking lot and the beach. The soaking rain made it difficult for either of them to see more than a few steps above or below, and Milty had to yell to be heard over the vociferous gale. A scream from Diane or Velma—he couldn't decipher which—floated past his ears, accompanied by a volley of sand and rain. The cries were carried from somewhere near The Fry Fry.

"Did you hear that?" Milty called to the man directly across from him.

Rex nodded. "Who was it?"

"Can't tell," Milty yelled in response. "But we need to help them. I think they might—"

The rain suddenly felt warmer, stickier. The lighting was poor, but he could see some dark streaks—rivers, really—starting to roll down Rex's face. Milty pulled his hat off and, even in the shadows, could recognize the blooming stain that'd begun to discolor the once-white foam dome.

"It's blood!" he said, dropping the cap at his feet.

Rex shook his head, clearly wanting it to not be true. He took a step backward, in the direction of the ocean, and Milty grabbed his arm.

"Where the hell are you going?"

Rex pointed toward the beach. "Anywhere. Anywhere but here, Man. I'm out."

The rain quickly rinsed the red from their faces, but Milty could feel his cheeks heating up with the developing rage he had for the other man. "But Diane and—and *Velma*. Your girlfriend. You're just gonna—what—leave her? To die?"

Rex took another step down but otherwise ignored the question. There was a second scream from somewhere in the dunes and both of their heads turned toward the sound.

Milty tried again. "Come on! You heard that, right? That's them. They need us!"

Rex held his hands out, keeping his palms flat and pointed upward. His long hair was drenched, and he looked like a wet, trembling Jesus. "I dunno, Man—I—"

"What don't you know?" Milty thought he might hit him. "Are you even listening? They need our help and—"

"We don't *know* who that is. We don't *know* whose blood just rained down onto us. Christ, Man. For all we know they're already dead!"

Milty leapt up and pushed him hard in the chest with both hands. "For all we know, they're *not*, you scumbag."

Rex shrugged and took another step away from him. "Yeah, well. *Sorry*," he said and then disappeared into the shadows. Milty lost sight of him after only a few stairs.

"You coward!" Milty shouted after him, but it was of no consequence. Rex wouldn't be changing his course of action. He wouldn't be turning around or coming back to help. Whatever happened next would be up to Milty to handle on his own.

What a chickenshit. Running off like a goddamned...chickenshit.

Determined that he wouldn't follow suit, Milty forced himself to turn around. Leaving his bloody hat where it lay on the platform, he began to creep back up the staircase. There was another scream—again he couldn't tell whose—and he quickened his pace. He didn't know who or what he might find at the top of the dunes, or in the parking lot, but he barreled on ahead just the same. He was a missile, blasting a path through the wind and rain—unceasing in its attempt to slow him—and stopped just as he crested the summit. Milty crouched down, trying his best to peer around the dunes and the whipping beach grasses, to see what awaited him in the parking lot.

Where are they?

The Fry Fry, only visible because of the light under its awning, winked at him through the monsoon. At first, he saw nothing else.

Where—?

And then, Diane and Velma toppled out from behind a knoll a few hundred yards away. They couldn't see him—he was still fairly well hidden—but it wouldn't have mattered. They were running for their lives.

Milty had just taken a step onto the pavement when the demon lowered itself between him and his two friends. Its back was to him and was turned toward Diane and Velma.

No!

They both skidded to a stop. Velma screamed and Diane tried to pull her back to safety. The Buoygeist began to fly in their direction, and Milty felt himself running toward it before he could stop himself or question whether or not there was a better—less hazardous—course of action.

"Hey, hey!" he heard himself screaming. "Over here! Look at me!" The experience was sort of a slow-motion, out-of-body one for him. He could see himself waving for the creature's attention, saw Diane's eyes widen as she recognized what he was doing, and then watched the monster pirouette through the raindrops like a murderous ballerina—a *Murderrina*, he laughed at his ill-timed joke—and face him.

"Ah, shit," he said aloud, realizing what he'd just brought upon himself. He opened his mouth again to hurl some curse at the thing when he finally noticed what it was holding in its non-harpoon hand.

Milty gagged.

Legs. Still clad in jeans, which were now almost entirely saturated in a dark red substance. Milty knew immediately who they'd belonged to.

Kyle.

Seeing that he had the thing's attention—and that Diane was, smartly, using the opportunity to drag Velma back into the dunes with her—Milty regained a bit of composure and howled. "You sick bastard! That's my friend—"

The Buoygeist interrupted whatever Milty'd been about to say by tossing Kyle's remains directly at him. Milty ducked—warm Kyle-splatter hitting him as the deceased whizzed by his head—just in time to see the demon lunging.

Right at me.

Milty folded himself into a ball and waited for death to find him.

CHAPTER THIRTY-FIVE

SURGE GARCIA

PLAY ▷

Behind A Dumpster

READY OR NOT, HERE Surge comes.

He'd been waiting for his opportunity—waiting for the ugly sonofabitch to show itself again. When Surge'd awoken on the pavement outside his shop, everyone else was gone. At first, he'd assumed the creature had finished them all off. There was no sign of the others and even he—with a flamethrower in hand—had been left severely wounded. Surge had a deep gash— which he couldn't see— down his back, and blood was leaking so badly from the top of his head that he had to keep wiping the stuff out of his eyes. Fortunately, the bandana he was already wearing served as the perfect bandage. He tightened that sucker just below where he thought the injury was, and soon enough the flow seemed to subside. It'd taken him a while to stand—nearly everything hurt—and by the time he was on his feet again, he saw the kids running up the staircase and toward the minimal shelter provided by The Fry Fry. He'd been about to call out when he saw what hunted them. Lurking. Just above the burger joint. He'd reacted by immediately throwing himself behind a nearby dumpster, from where he was able to observe everything that'd happened next. He'd witnessed the ensuing scatter—and, eventually, Kyle's grisly murder—unable to do anything to help.

And I just let that boy die. I just sat there. I just watched it happen.

Not that there was anything Surge could have done differently. His flamethrower was still lying uselessly in front of the storefront and, for all he knew, was too banged up to even work. He'd debated rushing for it but wanted to wait to see where the demon had gone. The night sky was darker than normal, making it nearly impossible for Surge to see where the evil was hiding.

But then the two girls—Diane and Velma—appeared from a dune just off the side of the lot. They were screaming when the demon appeared in front of them and Surge used the distraction to army crawl, the best he could, out to his old friend.

Wanda.

He picked her up, his hands bloody and shaking.

Wanda the flamethrower.

The tanks were still full, and he winced as he lugged the pack back on.

Hey, girl. Where you been?

But his happy reunion was short-lived. Diane and Velma were screaming. They needed his help and—

He spotted Milty crouching near the top of the staircase. Surge could tell what he was planning and gripped his weapon tighter, his forearms flexing in synchronicity with his jaw.

Don't do it, Son.

Milty stood up and began to wave his arms. The downpour and the deafening roar of the wind made it so that Surge could barely hear him, but that didn't matter. Milty had the thing's attention and it spun almost immediately.

Goddammit, Kid.

Unveiling its harpoon again, the Buoygeist lurched in the soaked moptop's direction. Inexplicably, the kid crouched down into a ball.

Run, dammit. What—what're you doing?

Surge watched the girls disappear again into the dunes and, as the cloaked leviathan flew toward its quarry, felt himself flick Wanda back on. She whirred to life, and he aimed her high into the air as he rushed out from behind his rusty garbage shield.

"Hey!" he heard himself screaming. "Hey, you piece of shit! Where you goin'? I've got somethin' for you!"

Wanda roared.

The Buoygeist screeched.

And, as the creature spun to meet his attacker, Milty ran. Towards the same hollow between the dunes the girls had crawled into.

Surge kept on throwin' flame. "Hey, remember me? Shoulda killed me when you had a chance! Ha, ha!"

Though the demon kept his eyes trained squarely onto Surge, he also lifted himself higher into the night to avoid any chance that his oily, dripping garment might somehow catch fire. The heinous spirit roared down from above as Surge and Wanda roared up, toward the heavens, from below. Out of the corner of his eye, without letting on that he spotted them, Surge noticed Milty, Diane, and Velma all running toward the staircase. Together. Back down toward the beach.

Hurry up! Go!

To give them more time, he continued letting it rip. The Buoygeist danced around, evading the pyrotechnics, but—at the same time—also refused to be scared away. It wanted Surge.

Surge released another burst of fire as the three disappeared down the stairwell, swallowed by shadow.

"Here I am, motherfucker!" Surge screamed. "That all you've got for me tonight? Huh? Show me what you—"

It was a flicker, barely catching an orange glimmer as it shuttled through the night, but Surge saw the seaweed-wrapped projectile just before it hit its mark. He screamed as he felt it go in, but Wanda's lament masked his own as he tumbled to the ground in front of his beloved Bay Video. And, as Surge fully began to grasp what'd happened, his eyes met a large yellow sign in his shop's window. His vision was blurring, but he knew exactly what those words implored him to do.

Be Kind. Please Rewind.

CHAPTER THIRTY-SIX

DIANE SHAW

PLAY ▷

Back On The Beach

SOMETHING STIRRED AT THE base of the dune.

"Don't move," Diane whispered.

The three of them kept their eyes trained on a small line of plastic erosion fencing. Hidden in the long grasses, and the even longer shadows, another rustle reached their ears. The flamethrower up above had suddenly gone quiet. Diane knew that wasn't a good sign for Surge.

Or for us.

Again. The grasses danced. Diane held out a finger, pointing to where the noise had originated from. Licking his lips like some fiend, Milty crept up to it. Diane hung back with Velma and waited.

"Be careful," she pleaded with him. Milty waved her off, but she urged caution again. "Milty. *Careful.*"

He didn't turn around. He reached his hand in and—

"Thought so," he muttered, dragging the drenched trust fund kid from the bushes. "It's just this *coward.*" He let the last word hang in the air. They all did.

Rex gesticulated somewhat ambiguously back in the direction of the stairs. "I—"

"You left us," Velma finished for him. "You left us to die."

"Hey, Velma—"

"Don't 'hey, Velma' me. If not for Milty, we'd all probably be dead right now. Just like Kyle and S—"

Milty shook his head, in denial. "We don't know yet about Surge. For all we know—"

"Milty..." Diane put a hand on his shoulder. That was enough to stop him.

The flamethrower is quiet. We all know what that means.

Diane rounded on Rex. "But, *maybe*—maybe if you hadn't only cared about your own ass—maybe Surge wouldn't have had to do what he did. There might have been something you could've done, some way you could've helped. Right? But we'll never know because you decided back there to only worry about *you*. We'll never know because you didn't even *try* to help."

Rex took a step back. Diane wasn't sure why, it wasn't as if they were any danger to him. But still, he shuffled closer to the dune and further from the group's reproachful gazes. "Oh, so now this—*all of this*—is somehow *my* fault? Get bent, Diane."

He turned to walk away. She watched his back for a moment before a thought dawned on her. In the chaos of the evening, she hadn't had an opportunity to fully flesh out the *why* of why everything unfolded in the way that it had. Something deep down made her, for a brief moment earlier on, even consider the possibility that she—in some unconscious desire to see Rex get what he deserved—had been the one to summon the creature. It'd shown up at her house first, after all.

No. Stop it, Diane. You know it wasn't you. You've known all along.

And Rex's sudden deflection of all blame for what'd occurred since their homecoming party on the beach had finally convinced her, assured her of what she hadn't an opportunity to be entirely confident of prior. It all made too much sense.

Blame, she thought. *Fault.*

Of course, it'd been Rex.

"Hey," she called out, still being quiet—still worried about drawing unwanted attention to their huddle. That thing was still out there, probably watching from up above in the black, never-ending abyss. They wouldn't see the next attack until it happened. "Hey," she called again, keeping her voice just barely audible. Rex stopped. "I know what happened."

Rex looked over his shoulder. "What?"

Neither Milty nor Velma spoke, but they both turned and looked at her.

"I know what *happened*," Diane repeated.

"What do you mean?" Milty asked, just above a whisper.

She pointed vaguely in the direction of the parking lot, Bay Video, and the demon. "I mean—I know who *called* it."

"Called it?" Milty still wasn't quite catching on. "The Buoygeist? But—Diane—you can't *call it*, right? I thought it sort of—"

"Shit, Milty," Diane massaged her forehead. *Why do you need to be so freaking literal all the time?* "You know what I mean. Not called it, but—whatever—*wanted* it. Summoned it. Use whatever verb makes you happy. Gimme a break, I'm not some word genius. Sorry if I'm—"

"No, no it's okay. I understand."

"What I'm saying is," Diane said, returning to the point of her message. "Is that I know who *wanted* this motherfucker. Kyle clearly was onto this earlier, but everything was moving too fast for us to really hear him. We didn't *listen*. It's taken me until just now—until I had a moment to stop, to breathe, and to think—to finally put the pieces together. But, now—now I *know*. And it's so obvious I could scream. I know who is to blame for all of this."

Velma stepped into their huddle so as not to have to speak too loudly. "I do too," she whispered, letting her eyes rise to meet her soon-to-be-ex's. "I know too."

CHAPTER THIRTY-SEVEN

REX TEMPLETON   PLAY ▷

Out Of The Shadows

LOSERS. AMAZING—ALMOST IMPOSSIBLE TO believe, really—that a town with such a deep, rich history could be home to such a collection of pedestrian, uninspired nitwits. What fortune to have grown up in the shadow of such greatness, such celestial awesomeness—and yet, these fools adorn themselves in ignorance and a lack of true appreciation for what bubbles just beneath the brackish surface of this—

"Rex," Velma was glaring at him. "I'm talking to you. It was you, wasn't it?"

He yawned, reached up, and pulled his "Be Wise" headband from where it collected his dreads. He shook his head and let his mane fall out around him. Absentmindedly, he stretched the bright blue elastic between his two hands—his brow furrowed, his eyes far away in deep thought—appearing to scrutinize it as he spoke. "Gosh, I'm—I guess, most of all—I'm just shocked it took you all so long to figure it out." He laughed. "I mean, *right*? How could it *not* have been me? Think about it. I practically *begged* you to take me to the damned thing and, Velma—Sunshine—I've been gabbing your ear off about this fucker since we got down here." He laughed again. "I guess, if we're gonna just rip the stupid band-aid clean off then, well, I guess I should probably inform you that, me and you—*us*—we might not have ever even happened if not for my fascination with *Him*. He really deserves all of the kudos for bringing the two of us together."

Velma's face was bright red. "You bastard. You—you *used* me?"

"No. I mean, well, *yes*—but, truthfully, I became quite fond of you. That was...*unexpected.*"

It wasn't my fault we ended up together in that Freshman Seminar class. It wasn't my fault you happened to be from the community I've been fixated on for so very long. Life happens. We happened.

"Why are you talking like that? Why do you sound...*different?*" She shook her head, realizing that was beside the point. "So, what..." Velma was still trying to piece his story together. Diane hovered behind her while Milty kept an eye focused on the sky, waiting for something to dive down and pluck the next one of them into the night. "You, like, searched me out? You, I dunno, *engineered* us finding each other, somehow?"

Oh gosh, no. That sounds like far too much work.

Rex rubbed his forehead, visibly exasperated that he had to explain everything to her. "Sunshine—"

"Stop," she held up a finger. "Stop calling me that."

"Fine. *Velma*," Rex started over. "It wasn't so complicated as all that, I assure you." He stretched his headband a bit more. "Look, it was more of a coincidence, if you can believe it. I forget exactly how it first came up in conversation, but the moment I realized where you were from, I realized—no, I *knew*—we needed to be together. I—"

Velma looked like she was about to vomit. She put a hand to her mouth. "This is sick. So effing sick. And, worst of all, it doesn't even make any sense. Like—*why?* Honestly. Explain it to me like I'm a four-year-old. You didn't need me, need us, to be able to come here. You could have put your grown ass on a bus or a plane or whatever and come here at your leisure. Why the need for, well, *everything* else? Why the...*game?*"

Is that all this is to you? A game?

Rex blew air out from his lips. "No, I didn't *need* you, per se. Don't give yourself quite so much credit. You're right, I already planned to make the trek myself in short order either way and—"

"Then, *why?*"

"Because you are *from* here. From this beautiful, cursed place. Being with you," he looked behind himself and shrugged as if he couldn't find the words to accurately describe his feelings. "Being with you was like carrying part of the story with me wherever I went. Being with someone from Eastham, the proverbial cradle of the sea devil, somehow made me feel a deeper connection to the legend. Brought me—*closer* to it. And I couldn't have predicted this, but I actually *fell* for you, Sunshine—"

"Don't."

"—and I hadn't planned for that. Truly. Fully. I fell in love with you, well before we ever got here, and—"

"Oh, please. *Stop.*"

"—despite what happened, and the animosity and negative vibes you're now sending my way, I still very much do."

They all stood in silence. Velma sniffed and calmly wiped a tear from one of her eyes. Diane squeezed her shoulder and Velma nodded a thanks.

"Want me to hit him?" Milty mumbled from the shadows.

Velma almost cracked a smile. "Nah. Not worth it. I don't want any of us to have to touch him—"

"Sunshine."

"—or breathe the same goddamned air—"

"Babe."

"—as this piece of shit, ever again."

"Hey, I told you I still love—"

Velma took a step closer, as if she really was planning to strike him. "Don't you *ever* say that word to me again." She started to cry harder and tears ran over her cheeks. "We *warned* you. We *told* you what would happen. We've lived here without a problem, forever. Our entire lives. And you brought this onto all of us. For *what*? Because of some little, sick obsession you have?"

"Sunshine."

"People *died*, Rex. Our friends *died*." She gritted her teeth. "And the night's not even fucking over."

Rex clasped his hands together. "Velma, listen to me. Our life together doesn't need to be over. We can survive this, *together*, and—"

She turned and started to walk away. Milty and Diane followed. "Just shut up."

"—bring *our* story to the rest of the world. Think of the publicity this could drum up. There's money in this. Movie deals. Book deals. The morning shows will all want to talk to us, to have us on. We could all—"

Thwump.

Rex grabbed his nose. Blood seeped between his fingers and he groaned. "What the hell, Diane?"

She shook her hand out. "Christ, that hurt." She turned to Velma. "Sorry, Vel. I know you didn't want us to touch him, but that sonofabitch wasn't ever going to shut his mouth."

Rex offered another muffled groan.

"Thanks, Diane," she took the other woman's injured hand and pulled her away. "Can we go? I don't want to be near him. Ever again."

Diane nodded and the two started climbing back into the dunes. Milty followed, without a word.

"Velma!" Rex pleaded loudly through his hand before remembering he shouldn't be screaming. He gasped, looking around, making certain he hadn't drawn too much attention to himself. He hissed after her once more, but Velma didn't respond. She didn't turn back around and—once the other three were fully devoured by the shadows—Rex decided he'd become too exposed. Too alone. He gave up begging and slunk backward into the grasses.

No point in chancing it. He smirked. *Like you said, Sunshine…the night's not even fucking over.*

CHAPTER THIRTY-EIGHT

MILTY BURKITTS PLAY▷

On A Dark Path

THERE WAS A SMALL trail further down the beach that provided an alternate route back up the dune. On that very path, Milty stood facing Diane. Velma was squatting on the ground, crying and lost in her own thoughts. Rain continued to pelt the three of them without any sign of letting up. Milty decided to try again.

"Please," he said. "He's up there. We're so close now. Already like—almost halfway up the hill. I just want to see—I just need to make sure."

"Milty—"

"I know, I *know* it's a long shot. How *could* he be alive, right? I get it. But don't we owe it to him to at least...*check*?"

Diane put one hand on each of his shoulders. She stepped closer and, for a brief moment, Milty thought she was going to kiss him. A droplet of water hung from the very tip of her sunburned nose and wiggled itself until it slid past her lips. A few strands of hair were plastered against her forehead and, despite the rain, she still wore her Drive-In cap backward. The informal look left her appearing more laid-back, more relaxed, and not nearly as serious as her otherwise sober tone and demeanor would've had him believe. That night had been hell, and he knew Diane had trudged through it all alongside him, but—for a brief instant—he lost himself in the nonchalance of her inexplicably reversed hat.

"Listen to me," she said, allowing her eye contact to linger. He could feel the moisture escape from her mouth and touch his face, and he breathed it in deeply. "Surge made his decision. If we stumble back up there now—it could make his sacrifice a waste. For nothing."

Milty didn't brush her hands away and continued to lock eyes with her. "I need to know, Diane. *For sure.*"

She sighed. "You know, we only have to get through a couple more hours, Man. A couple more hours until daylight and then—that thing—"

"I know," he stopped her. "I know. It'll be gone. Just a couple more hours." He bit his lip. "And yet..."

Please, Diane.

Diane closed her eyes. "I'm not going to be able to convince you, am I?"

Milty took the opportunity, without her looking, to examine the freckles on her cheeks and the way her nostrils flared as she waited for him to respond. She *was* cute, and he found himself wondering why his brain hadn't ever articulated that exact thought before. "Well," he said. "Probably not. But you know you don't *have* to come with me, right? You could hang here with Vel. I'd be right back."

Diane looked down to Velma. Though she was still not participating in their conversation, she should easily have been able to hear them at that distance. "I guess there's nothing to say we're safer staying here, in the dunes, is there?"

Milty shrugged. "And, if you're right—if Surge is..." he couldn't finish the sentence. "Well, then—at least we'll be back up top. Near the shop. Near his bunker."

Diane nodded, her face scrunched up in thought. "And that would be a better place to ride out these last coupla hours."

Milty raised his eyebrows. "So, you in then?"

Diane squatted down beside Velma. "What do you think, Vel?"

Velma, tears streaking her face, stammered. "I—I—I don't want to stay out here any longer." She stood up. "Let's go."

Diane rose with her. "Well, alright then. That answers that." She punched Milty in the shoulder. "Lead the way."

Is she—is she flirting?

Milty smiled. It didn't make any sense; there wasn't much to smile about, but he did regardless.

Weirdest first date ever. He shrugged and spun to face the ascending, unlit path. *Here we come, Surge. Ready or not.*

CHAPTER THIRTY-NINE

SURGE GARCIA

PLAY ▷

Inside A Dumpster

EVERYTHING REEKED. EVERYTHING HURT. Surge flickered in and out of consciousness. He couldn't see much at all, but whether or not that was because the lid of the dumpster was shut tightly or because his vision was cutting in and out, he couldn't tell. In fact, how he'd even managed to pull himself out of the night and into safety, remained a little fuzzy.

The demon's harpoon had pierced directly into his thigh and came out somewhere under his ass. He couldn't tell if it'd hit any major arteries, but there *was* a ton of blood, and what'd started as a sizable flood became a gushing deluge when he yanked the crude barnacle-covered javelin out with his bare hands. The decision to do so must have happened fast—immediately, even—as the creature hadn't a chance to attack again before Surge clambered into the open trash receptacle and slammed the heavy top shut.

I know you're out there, yah bastahd.

There was a small sliver of light he could peek through.

I know you still want a piece of 'ol Surge.

He nodded.

Once and for all. You want me gone.

He shook his head and almost cried out. Even that small amount of movement was excruciating for him.

But tonight isn't that night. Tonight, I'm still here. I'm still here, still ready to—

There it was. Drifting nearby. Hovering a few feet off the ground. Just outside the dumpster. And though there was a significant and consistent gusting of wind, the devil's frock didn't acknowledge any external forces. Even as the creature revolved around him, the blackened, shriveled material that covered and hid its frame barely registered a ripple. In any case, the thing continued its circling of the trash prison, as if it were uncertain of exactly where Surge had escaped to.

Like a dumb dog playing fetch. I threw that tennis ball, but he's too stupid to know for sure where it went.

Surge tried to shift, and the large hole in his leg sent a shock wave of white-hot agony radiating up into his torso. He stifled a scream by biting his tongue, immediately tasting copper.

Shit, shit, shit, shit. Got to do somethin', Surge. Those kids need ya.

Something warm and juicy seeped into the back of his pants. It could've been wet garbage warmed by the sun. Could've been a festering raccoon carcass. Could've been his body draining of blood and other vital fluids. Whatever it was, it was gnarly.

Think, Asshole, think. If you jump outta here too quickly, that thing's gonna nab ya and you're gonna die. If you sit in here too long, you're likely to bleed to death.

He was about to take another gander outside when—

Screeeeeeeeeeeech.

It was taunting him. Why the Buoygeist didn't just rip the top off the dumpster and fish him out was impossible to know.

It's 'cause he wants you to run. He wants to hunt your Moby Dick ass like a zombie Captain Ahab.

He saw it shift outside again, a shadow silhouetted by other shadows.

Screeeeeeeeeeeech.

Surge gritted his teeth. He considered giving the beast what it wanted. He was going to die soon anyway, so why not go out in a blaze of glory?

Because that's not helping anyone, old timer. Those kids might still be alive. What you gotta do is hang on just a little longer, in case they—

The shadow moved again, this time fully disappearing out of view. Surge strained to listen. He heard something, not the demon dragging its lance across his rusted metal cocoon but—something else.

Voices. Yes. I hear—

Whispering. Sneakers scraping along the wet pavement. The door to the shop opening and then the *click-clack* of the lock.

They were okay. At least some of them were.

Surge dared to keep peeking. He was alone, or at least appeared to be. He let his eyes scan the ground circling his blue, stinking, hideaway.

Where are you—?

And then he saw her.

Wanda.

For an instant, he thought he might dive out, dramatically tumble across the blacktop like Stallone, and retrieve her. But, rather quickly, he gave up his visions of heroism and grandeur. He was an old man—a heavily bleeding old man at that—and he didn't have the energy to do anything but plop back down onto his trash bag divan and let his eyes continue to get heavy.

Just don't die, he begged himself. *That's all you can do right now. Just don't die.*

Chapter Forty

Milty Burkitts

PLAY ▷

Bay Video (Back In The Basement)

Click-clack.

The three of them gathered in Surge's basement bunker. Diane immediately began searching the shelves for something to eat—there was enough canned food to last at least a month, it looked, though no obvious sign of a can opener. Velma flopped down on the cot and buried her face into the green, woolen army blanket.

We're safe now. Milty reassured himself but then realized he hadn't offered the sentiment aloud. "We're safe now. Let's all just take a breath for a minute and figure things out."

"Breaths taken," Diane mumbled without turning away from the cans. "Multiple breaths. That said, if I don't find a mother-effin' opener soon, I'm going to need to borrow your teeth, Milty."

He couldn't be certain she wasn't serious and absently let his tongue cover up his rather large central incisors.

"How do you know we're safe?" It was Velma, still face-down on the cot.

Milty stood in front of the storm door, which was locked tightly behind him. "Well," he fumbled for a good answer. "Well, I guess I don't know for sure. But there are now multiple layers of doors for this thing to bust through, and—and who's to say it even saw us come in here? Right? I didn't see it out there, did you? Plus, it didn't even attempt to get in at us the last time we were down here. I—yeah, I'm fairly confident we're okay now."

No, you're not.

He took a quick peek over his shoulder after a particularly loud gust of wind battered the building from up above.

You're most definitely not.

"A-ha!" Diane exclaimed from her perch in front of the shelving unit. "Not a can-opener, but I did find an unopened box of Octo-O's."

Octo-O's was an obscure, off-brand cereal—complete with tiny, sugar-coated octopi—that was only sold down Cape. Milty had always hated it. Tasted like—

Styrofoam.

That's what he'd always thought.

Stale styrofoam. And toothpaste.

He cringed. "I'll pass."

Diane offered some to Velma, but she too declined the Cape Cod delicacy. Diane shrugged. "Hey, suit yourself. More for me." She dug a hand inside the box and began bringing large piles of the stuff to her mouth. Individual little purple octopi tumbled down her shirt and onto the floor. She seemed to barely notice.

Milty puttered around. "I just feel like we should be doing something."

Diane shook her head. "Nossir. We don't even need to wait all that long. Sun's up soon and then this nightmare is over. There's nuthin' more we need to do. Just hunker down and...wait this out."

Milty let his eyebrows rise and fall. Hopefully, it'd be enough of a response to her assertion. He didn't have the energy for a more robust rebuttal. He sat down at Surge's desk and began to distractedly open drawers and investigate the inner contents. Old photographs, stacks of stapled-together receipts, some newspaper clippings that hadn't yet made it onto the wall, and—

"Hold up," Milty muttered. "Guys. I found something."

Diane was still fixated on a fistful of Octo-O's. "Gonna hafta be more specific," she said through an overflowing mouth.

Milty spun around to share his discovery with the other two, though Velma still clearly wasn't interested in playing ball. She didn't even open her eyes. "Hey, take a look at this," he continued. "Some sort of journal. And it's most *definitely* in Surge's handwriting."

Diane laughed. "So, *what*—now we're thumbing through the old man's diary? Nah, no thanks. Nope. I'm not that bored yet."

Milty ignored her. "No, it's—it's not like that. This is—uh, well—covered in bloody fingerprints to begin with. Ick." Diane lifted a single eyebrow and he kept on going. "But, more importantly, it's filled with notes. His notes. It's...it's all about the Buoygeist."

That got Diane's attention. "Huh? Is it now?"

Milty kept flipping through. "Ya, it makes sense. He said he'd been waiting for this thing, didn't he? He's—" Milty gestured toward the wall of newspaper clippings. "He's obviously been doing his own research. For a long, *long* time."

Diane stood beside him, trying to read over his shoulder. "Here, scoot over," she commanded. "You got a tiny butt, make some room."

Milty felt himself flush at the thought of her checking out his rear, but he obliged. Together they shared the small desk chair. "Yeah, there's *a lot* here," he scanned the pages. "And it's so well organized too. There are pages on suspected victims, connected news stories, past investigations that went nowhere, and—hmm, well, that's interesting."

Diane tried to get a look at what he was seeing. "What is it?"

Milty felt the heat in his cheeks a little more, realizing how close Diane was to him. He could smell her sweat and found himself not minding it in the slightest. "I—uh," he tried to unscramble his thoughts. "Well, um, at the back. On the very last page, he—*Surge*—theorizes about how to get rid of it."

Diane sat up. "But don't we already know that? The sun comes out and it disappears back into its hole or whatever. Right?"

Milty shook his head. "Well, yes and no. When the sun comes up, it does *retreat*. Back to the place it comes from. To rest, or whatever, until some idiot shows up and disturbs it all over again. But, this—" he tapped excitedly at the page. "This is different. This, right here, is Surge theorizing on how to eradicate this thing, like...*forever*."

Diane blinked. "Like, how to *kill* it?"

Milty rubbed a hand across the stubble forming on his chin. He could tell Diane was watching him do it but pretended not to notice. "Exactly. Surge thinks—or he writes—that the demon escapes back into its own dark hell because he can't deal with the light. With daybreak."

Diane still didn't understand. Her head swayed back and forth as she tried to figure out what he was saying. "Ok, so..."

"So," Milty continued. "Surge simply asks the question: What if it *doesn't* make it back to its sanctuary? What if it *doesn't* manage to get itself back down to the anchor, back down below the buoy? What *then?*"

Diane chewed on her bottom lip. "I get what you're—what *he's*—saying, but, realistically, how would anyone be able to stop it?"

Milty read further before answering. "Shit," he said, suddenly looking up, his face exuding incredulity. Milty stared at Diane. "He *swam* down there."

"Who, Surge?"

Milty nodded. "Yeah. Yes. That's what he says here. Says he pulled himself down the chain. From the buoy to the sea floor. Scuba gear and all. Says there's something down there...like an...'an ancient manhole cover' he says. He thinks, *if* there's a way to close it—"

"There's a way to kill it," Diane finished for him.

Milty and Diane looked at one another. After a second, he picked up her hand and squeezed it. "It's all well and good, but—easier said than done."

From the cot, Velma, breathing her unease with what they were discussing, finally spoke up. "We wouldn't even make it out of the shop, never mind all the way back to the marina. *No way.* Please. We need to just ride this out. We'll go to the police in the morning and—"

"The *police?*" Milty said, closing the journal. "You think they don't already know about this thing? Dammit, Vel, they've been hiding the truth for years, decades, *shit*—probably *centuries* for all we can tell. It makes sense, *financial* sense, for them to keep this quiet and keep their precious tourism industry booming. They'll never, *ever* acknowledge what's down there," he squeezed Diane's hand tighter and she squeezed back. "No matter how much chaos and death it brings."

Velma was sitting up again, her blond hair scattered about her face. It looked like she'd just ridden with her head out a car window for some distance. The bags under her eyes were a deep shade of purple—like some terrible, dollar-store eyeshadow—and she trembled. All over. Her lips, her hands, her knees. "Please," she implored them. "Don't make me go back out there. Not until—"

Click-clack.

There was a sound from above.

Click-clack.

Again. The front door unlocking and then locking again.

"Why would it—?" Milty stopped speaking when he heard something bringing itself down the stairs. One shuffle step. Then another. Slowly.

"Get back," he whispered to the other two. "Find something to defend yourself with."

The doorknob on the storm door turned and then shuddered. There was a weak scratch, followed by a dragging sound. From the top of the doorway to the bottom. Slowly sliding.

Thwump.

All went quiet. Milty crept to the door. He pressed his ear to it and listened.

"Son?"

Milty jumped backward, clutching his chest. "Surge? Is that—?"

Diane rushed in front of him. "Of course, it's him, Dummy. Open the damn door." And she pulled it wide.

"Surge!" both he and Diane said in unison. They knelt on the floor and pulled him into the room. Milty quickly slammed the door shut and bolted it again once the opening was clear. In his arms, the old man clutched his trusty flamethrower, Wanda. "How—how're you—?"

"What, *alive?*" he laughed, hacking up a wad of phlegm and bloody mucus. It was clear he was in rough shape. Each breath he took was labored, his eyes were bouncing all over the place, and he was soaked with perspiration. As he spoke to them, he smiled the best he could. "I got lucky, kids. A little angel must've been on my shoulder tonight. Hopefully still hanging out there a little longer, too. I know I don't look so hot, but I'm still here. Someone out there wanted me to live, at least a little bit longer. Because we all still have very important work to do tonight."

Milty and Diane helped him to sit up, while Velma remained on the cot. Her eyes were wide, her complexion taking on a ghostly pallor. "What work?" she asked, terrified.

"Ha!" Surge hacked again. His eyes were about at desk level, and he noticed his journal lying just out of reach. "I see you've been doin' some light reading. You all know what it is we need to do then, don't you?"

Milty stood up. He pressed the glow feature on his digital watch and then nodded. "We got about an hour until sunrise. Who's driving?"

CHAPTER FORTY-ONE

DIANE SHAW

PLAY ▷

Surge's Truck

THE WIPERS CRANKED.

Flip. Flip. Flip. Flip.

It was still pouring out. All four of them were crammed into the small cab of Surge's baby blue, 1970 Ford F-100 pickup. He'd insisted on taking the wheel—*no one drives my Maria, but me*—and Diane cringed, wondering to herself why the man insisted on naming all of his possessions after his failed relationships.

Doesn't matter. Eyes on the prize, Diane. Eyes on the prize.

She was squeezed in tightly beside Surge, Velma next to her, and Milty was against the passenger side window. Surge's lap was soaked, leaking really, and he kept catching himself—his eyes flickering, his head nodding a tad too close to the dashboard—as if he were, more than once, about to lose consciousness. Each time he started to droop, Diane would reach for the wheel, but he would shoot straight up and push her hand away. "No, no. *Nope,*" he'd insisted. "I'm good. I'm good. Surge is good. Surge is here. Not dead yet."

Yet, Diane tensed. *But if you pass out while you're driving...*

"Hey, look," Milty pointed as they flew past the Drive-In. "Emergency vehicles everywhere. They're gonna have a hard time creating an alternative storyline for this one."

Surge cackled, wiping something wet from his face at the same time. "Oh, you think so? Is *that* what you think? Hah. Well, you're damn wrong, Kid. You're *damn* wrong. These people—these sick, twisted people—they already got plenty of stories all banked up, concocted, and ready to go. Even this—even this fiasco—they'll be able to explain away. They always find something. Mass hallucination or some shit. And, if need be, they'll resort to lockin' up folks who refuse to keep silent. You'll see. They'll pay you off or they'll send you off. Whatever it takes to keep the status quo and the news stations away." He hit the accelerator and put the blue and red flashers in the rearview mirror.

They were speeding, and Diane kept looking behind them, making sure they hadn't been followed. "It's weird, isn't it?"

"What?" Velma asked, still with them. She'd put up quite a fight, begging them all to stay in the basement until sunrise, but—in the end—also didn't want to be left alone.

Diane's chin was resting on the cushion in front of the small sliding cab window. "I guess I can't believe we didn't see it. You know? We left the basement, and it was just...*gone*."

Surge's hands tightened around the rawhide steering wheel cover. "Oh, don't fool yourself. He's not gone. He's just...*waiting* for his chance. Didn't enjoy 'ol Wanda, I'd wager." He gestured behind them in the bed of the truck. "Think she probably just bought us a little extra time."

Diane could see Wanda sliding and bouncing with each little rut or pothole the truck hit. She wouldn't do them any good while they drove. She was out there and they were all—

In here.

Milty cleared his throat as if he were about to make an important speech to the troops. "Hey, so, we're getting close. We'll be at the marina in a few minutes. We all good with the plan? We'll need to do this fast. In and out, right?"

Surge ran a red light and then turned left off of Route 6 onto a side road. He repeated what they'd all already agreed to. "I take you out in the rowboat. You'll be our diver—" he pointed at Milty. "—you'll pull that sucker, the cover, back over the hole, and the girls will stand guard with Wanda on the dock."

Diane sighed. It made no sense for Surge to be out in the rowboat with Milty. He could barely keep himself awake and would be

far more helpful wielding the flamethrower, which she and Velma
hadn't ever even touched. She'd argued the point but hadn't been
listened to.

"Surge are you sure—?"

He nodded his head vociferously. There would be no debate.
"Look, once that thing sees what we're up to, he's gonna come
howlin' in like an intercontinental ballistic missile. The person in
most danger will be the asshole sitting unprotected in that little
dingy. I'd prefer, if you don't mind, that the asshole be *me*. The old
man who's already on the way out." He grazed his leg and winced.
The pain was clearly getting to him. Diane was impressed by how
well he'd somehow been able to press on. And despite her concern
with his ability to even get himself *in* the rowboat, she did appreciate
that he was putting himself in—what he believed to be—the most
dangerous, most vulnerable position, rather than asking anyone else
to do so.

"Okay, okay," she put her hands up. "I understand. You're the
boss."

Surge pulled onto the marina road. It was dirt-covered and went
on for some distance. A large wooden sign at the marina entrance was
just barely visible on the horizon.

Almost there.

Diane sighed and returned her gaze to the back of the truck. A
shadow shifted overhead, behind them in the dark. What looked like
a stagnant, slow-moving cloud in one moment, suddenly lurched
closer to their vehicle in the next. Diane felt the hair stand on her
forearms and the back of her neck. Without removing her eyes, and
refusing to blink, she warned the others. "It's here."

Surge didn't need to ask any other questions. He hit the gas even
harder. They barreled toward the main gate.

"Where is it?" Velma squealed.

Diane scanned the blackness behind them. Rain peppered the
glass and made it hard for her to see much at all. "I—I'm not sure
where—"

"Hurry, Surge," Milty said from the other side of the cab.

"I'm hurrying, Kid. Doing what I can do. If I go any faster, we'll
come in too hot and end up leaping off that pier into the harbor."

The truck's engine roared.

Diane continued to search for any indication of where it'd gone, but she couldn't find it. She couldn't see anything.

Where are you?

The truck was less than a football field's length away from the main entrance to the marina. The headlights lit the sign up. It hadn't been long since they'd all last been there, but it felt to Diane like a lifetime had gone by.

Where are you, you sonofa—

Velma put a hand on her shoulder. "Diane, do you see—?"

Crrrruncccch, sllllluuuurck.

Velma gurgled. The harpoon had gone directly through the cab's roof, piercing Velma just under her collarbone. She was pinned to the seat and flailed as blood began to spurt against the windshield.

"Shit!" Milty screamed next to her.

Diane touched the spear. "Oh, my God. Hold, on Vel. Hold on."

Surge hit the brakes, but it was too late. An unseen force barreled into the side of the truck and sent it rolling—down into the embankment just before the entrance to the marina. As each side of their vehicle connected with the man-made rock wall that lined the road, they were serenaded by *crunch*es and *cronk*s and the *crink*ling of glass as it showered down onto their heads.

"Hold on!" Surge bellowed.

Diane covered Velma the best she could and braced for impact.

CHAPTER FORTY-TWO

VELMA GREEN

PLAY ▷

The Marina

EVERYTHING AROUND HER WAS dim. Distorted. Muffled voices from far away called her name, pleaded with her to move, to speak, to stop heading in the direction her tired—her so, so tired—brain petitioned to her go. Velma only wanted to rest. Her eyelids were heavy, and it felt so good to let them just *close*.

Just a few more minutes, Mom. That's all I need. Just a few more minutes.

The garbled cries were what kept her from drifting off fully. That and the tendrils of thick, acrid smoke that licked and danced into her flared, blood-encrusted nostrils. Velma coughed and then she choked. On the black flumes. On the liquid that burbled up from her insides and out through her wide-open mouth. On the fear that enveloped her as she became more alert, more awake, and remembered where she was.

H-h-h-help.

There was a pressure building in Velma's head. She was upside down and unable to move. Someone was still in the cab with her, pushing. Someone else was outside—pulling. Her hands, shaking, found their way to the large object that protruded from her chest—still holding her tightly to the leather cab seat, restricting her ability to move or breathe—and she sobbed as she touched it. Though she was conscious, she could only imagine—considering how much blood was in the process of leaving her—that it wouldn't be long before everything around her evaporated into sudden darkness. She hoped, when that inevitably happened, that it'd all just melt away and that she wouldn't feel it. She wanted it to be quick and painless—pleasant even—like a breeze sneaking in through an open window on a summer night. But something told her that line of thinking was wishful.

"Time to go!" someone instructed her. Whoever spoke was in charge, confident, but also allowing himself to be as gentle as his voice—and the circumstances—would permit.

Surge.

"Up and at 'em! Come on now. Here we go. We've got to—" His hands were trying to pull her free, but the force with which the harpoon had been thrown made it impossible to jostle her loose. "Milty, Son, grab her leg!"

Velma was fading in and out. She could sense Milty beside her, but his face was all swirly and kaleidoscope-y. Like an apparition in a carnival fun-house mirror, he spoke to her. "Hey, Vel. Hey, hey. Stay with us. We're gonna get you outta here."

Nice of you to think so optimistically.

She felt more warmth bubble over her lips and gagged, spitting out even more of her insides. "It hurts."

"I know," he said, looking over his shoulder. The flames were getting pretty high and made it hard to see what was happening on the other side of the glass. "I think we just need to—"

A scream from outside made her eyes open all the way again. It was Diane. "Guys! We've got to go! Now! It's—it's *coming*!"

Diane shrieked. Something massive crunched down on top of the exposed side of the truck, and Velma watched as Diane pulled Milty away. "N-n-n-no," he protested, attempting to re-enter the vehicle. "We can't just—"

Surge pushed him back. "You both get the hell outta here. I'll get her. But you—*run*. There's no time. Go! Now!"

Milty and Diane disappeared, leaving Velma alone in the cab with Surge. The enclosure was almost completely filled by a gray cloud, but she could see his large eyes soften. The creases on the sides of his face spider-webbed outward as he held back some obvious distress.

He put a hand to her head. "Ok. Here we go, Kid. On the count of—"

"Don't leave me," she pleaded. "Please."

He shook his head. "Hey, now. I promise I won't. I'm not going—"

Surge's eyes went wide when the demon grabbed his ankle. Ripped from the vehicle, Velma caught only a glimpse of him—a blur, really—flying through the air. His body crashed, limply, through the marina sign. Milty and Diane both screamed, but his shape—a nondescript shadow, quiet and decommissioned—didn't appear to stir at all in response.

Oh, please, no.

And, through the smoke, a face appeared. At first, Velma thought the meaty appearance shimmered, like glossy wrapping paper. But then, up close, she could see that what she mistook as *shimmering* was actually the *slithering* of thousands of leeches as they fought for territory on the face of her executioner. Its countenance, still locked in a preposterous forever-smile—like a long-decaying circus clown—leered over her as the creature slunk inside the cab, filling the tiny space with its sludge-covered robes and an overwhelming, sour stench of festering sea life. As it grabbed a hold of its harpoon and her—and pulled the both of them from the truck—she felt her own life beginning to slide away. Down, down, down, down. Wavy lines flickered, as did her vision, and she quickly realized the pain was also fading.

Her body lifted. The truck was now below her. Beside it, two overwrought, horrified faces stared up at her, acknowledging the truth of her predicament.

Milty and Diane.

They both waved their arms, their mouths stretched wide open. They beckoned her—beckoned *it*—pleading for their friend's safe return, but she could not hear them, and *it* would not listen. She could not hear *anything* anymore, would never again, and *it* did not care.

The demon pulled her body from the harpoon and the harpoon from her body. And, as she fell toward the earth, she caught one last glimpse of her friends. Their faces were wet, not from the rain that fell all around them, but from the imposed, gratuitous pain that witnessing such carnage had branded them with.

Velma opened her mouth to call out, but her last breath came and went. The world went dark, and—before hitting the ground—she felt it all just *melt away*.

CHAPTER FORTY-THREE

MILTY BURKITTS PLAY ▷

On The Dock

IT WAS AN ORANGE sliver. A thin line on a dark, dark backdrop. Though the rain hadn't yet fully stopped, the fiery wedge had begun to split across the horizon, as if the diabolism of that evening was beginning to gradually weaken, crumble, and break apart. Spokes of light crept out from behind the Buoygeist's cowl, like an obscene halo, as it stared down at the crumpled ruin that had once been Velma Green. Like a puppy that'd played too hard with its chew toy, it seemed to wonder—with a cockeyed neck lean—what it'd done to its once squeaky plaything.

Run!

Milty didn't know if the voice was in his head, if it came from Diane, or if it was the entreaty from Surge somehow still floating on the ether, co-mingling with the straggling raindrops—the last vestiges of the storm they'd all endured. What he did know was that he *would* listen to it. He would *not* turn around. He would not stop his feet from *moving*.

We know what has to be done.

His hand was in Diane's. After pulling him from the car, she hadn't detached. Linked in one another's bloody grasp, they barreled down the dock toward the cold murkiness that awaited them both. Their feet pounded on the wooden slabs, echoing onto the creek—and into the night—a broadcast of their intentions.

What has to be done.

The demon howled. Their end game was clear, and they'd been spotted in the act.

"Don't look back!" Diane implored through gulps of salty, near-morning air. "Whatever you do, don't stop!"

His fingers clasped hers so tightly that he thought bones were surely close to breaking. But she squeezed back just as hard—*harder*—and pulled him along with her. Milty stumbled and Diane caught him, preventing him from landing flat on his face. In the process, they both saw it bearing down on them. Torpedoing toward the end of the dock, its harpoon hefted and ready to gut. Its smile—a bloody, gaping, festering incision—caterwauled from over their frantically scampering forms, like a red-tailed hawk attempting to scare its prey out of hiding. And, as it descended, the banshee's sodden, begrimed cloak *flap, flap, flap, flap*ped a portent of its approach.

"Diane!" Milty cried as the shadow overtook them. "Diane, it's—"

"I know," she cut him off, in stride, refusing to look. "Get ready to jump!"

"Diane, it's—"

"One..."

"—here!"

"Two..."

"Diane!"

"Three!"

Sllllfffffft.

Milty felt the bite behind his leg. A white-hot slice across his Achilles. Something flapped loose and wet across his calf, spurting as he tumbled hard onto the dock. Diane was airborne, and he heard her splash a distance away, cloaked by inky foam and bubbles. Milty rolled to his stomach and started to desperately drag himself back toward the end of the dock, but he knew he wouldn't make it.

"Diane!" he screamed. "Diane, he's coming!"

But she wouldn't hear him. Diane was already deep beneath the waves. The Buoygeist disregarded its injured quarry and instead hovered briefly over the surface of the channel, reeds of seagrasses waving to the devil in welcome. It lowered its hooded face toward the ripples, tracking its new prey—following Diane as she swam underwater toward her target, which bobbed tranquilly in the middle of the creek.

The buoy.

And then, just as it came to brood over its place of origin, the specter dove.

Hurry, Diane.

And the orange from behind Milty began to grow. The sky was catching fire, the evil beginning to burn off with the advent of the sun.

Hurry.

Morning was coming.

CHAPTER FORTY-FOUR

DIANE SHAW

PLAY ▷

Beneath The Waves

AT FIRST, THE NEAR complete absence of light had been disorienting to Diane. Though she was deep under the surface, her eyes were opened wide. It stung, but, having grown up in the salt and sand of Cape Cod, Diane had practically lived in the water. In the ocean. Her hair was perpetually stiffened and bleached by the bay, and if it'd been left up to her, she'd have spent every waking hour of every day surfing and lying on the beach. Surfing and lying on the beach. Rinse and repeat. What else could she possibly need in life?

Milty—

The name popped into her brain even as the air gradually began to leak from her lungs. She could hold her breath for an extended period, but she'd already gone a good distance without breaching. She continued to pull herself through the surprisingly strong current before the rest of the answer revealed itself.

—and horror movies.

Bubbles flew past her face as she searched for her mark. She had no way of knowing how close Milty was to her, but she hoped he wasn't too far. She was a better swimmer than him—always had been—which is why she'd been so taken aback when he and Surge decided she would be more helpful to them on the dock. In the end, it hadn't mattered, but—even at her current depth—part of her still bristled that she'd been so easily overlooked.

Can't be much farther. I have to be close.

If Diane didn't find the buoy soon, she'd be forced to surface for air. She scanned her surroundings, noticing some incremental lightening.

The sun. Dawn. It's almost here.

She swam faster.

Hurry, Diane. You need to get there first.

And then, just as she was about to give up and return for a gulp of air, she spotted it.

A chain.

Red. Rusted.

She knew what it was the second she saw it. Diane reached for the deep-sea shackle and immediately began to pull herself down. Down, down, down, down. Link by link, hand over hand, she dragged herself to the bottom of the creek bed. The pressure was increasing with each passing moment, with each readjustment and tug. She was almost there and nearly out of breath.

You can't quit now, D. You have to finish this.

As the thought left her brain, she noticed a flat circular object growing in size as she approached the seabed. Just at the base of the chain, there was a large stone slab with indecipherable etchings carved onto it—like some ancient Mesopotamian manhole cover. A thick layer of periwinkle and other crustaceans was littered across it, making the thing nearly impossible to read. And, right beside that, was a human-sized opening.

Oh my God.

It was a yawning, sepulchral abyss, and—as she dragged herself closer—heard, emanating from its open jaws, wails that could only have come from the most afflicted, the most tormented of souls. As Diane reached the precipice of the chasm, the screams became nearly unbearable for her to listen to. Pleading for her to take notice, agonized laments bore into her ears and—eventually—into her skull, as if she were placing her head directly beside a speaker at a Black Sabbath concert.

"Hellllp ussss, sssssssiiiinner."

No, stop.

"Find usssssss."

"Freeeee usssssssss."

She covered her ears and thrashed in an attempt to escape the overtures.

"Want ussssss."

"Bleeeeeed ussssssss."

Stop!

"Killllll usssssssssssssssssss."

Hurry! Do it!

She lunged for the cursed manhole cover. Her lungs on fire. Placing both hands on either side of it she lifted and—

No. No, no, no, no.

It wouldn't budge. She had no idea of what material the object was crafted from, but she doubted even Milty and Surge would've been any help in moving it. The weight was incredible, and she knew right away she was not going to be able to shift it back into place over the hole. She looked back toward the opening of the demon's prison.

Dammit. Think, think, think, think.

The choir continued its song.

"Flessshh, we want—"

No!

"Tear, bite, sllllllice—"

Please!

"Warm juiccesssss—"

Stop, stop, stop, stop!

"—pour from our lipsssss—"

Diane let go of the sides of the giant cover. She had no more time.

"—over its chin—"

No!

"Tassssstes like deathhhh."

Diane was close to passing out. Her vision was wavering. She needed air and fast. And then—just then—she caught something approaching out of the corner of her eye.

God, no.

It was rocketing toward her. Trickles of sunlight danced around it, but the Buoygeist was coursing through the waves and would be on her in seconds. Even at a distance, there was now enough light to see that its smile was starting to finally fade. To survive and to be reincarnated again for another cycle of murdering, it would need to return to its watery grave. Before daybreak. And Diane was trying to stop that from happening.

It knows what I'm doing.

She saw its grin slowly metamorphosing into a terrified, comprehending grimace.

And it's scared.

Diane blinked. Even that far under, she blinked.

Which means...which means Surge was right. This—this could actually work.

Diane knew what she had to do. There was no other option. If she rose to the surface to get air, the demon would disappear back into the hell it had come from, safely protected until the time came that it was summoned once again.

Okay, then.

And Diane moved. Bringing herself directly over the opening, she hesitated for a moment with both of her feet braced on either side of it. She made eye contact with the approaching creature, who bellowed out a torrent of bubbles and a black, inky spew in protest.

Now.

Diane dropped herself in. The hole was just about her size—surprisingly small considering the gargantuan being that'd exploded out of it—and she plugged it up nicely. In fact, as she attempted to wriggle herself in even lower, she realized she was firmly stuck. Her hip bones dragged on whatever stone lined the inside of the hole, and she gritted her teeth, fully prepared and bracing herself for what happened next.

A flash of metal, spiraling through the current, pierced through her stomach and—before she even fully registered what'd happened—exited out her back. She watched as blood began to leak from the gash in her abdomen and marveled as it danced with the fingers of light that'd managed to breach the deepest recesses of the marina and welcome Diane and her assailant to the new day.

It was then that she began to lose consciousness.

And the harpoon disappeared into the murky depths, a few harmless bubbles trailing after it.

And the demon's face—snarling and locked in a crazed scream—began to shed pieces of itself. Chunks of barnacle and leathered, meaty jowls, framed by a black hood that trembled and seesawed in the ebb and flow of the current, started to plunge toward the sediment and the ocean floor. The pieces scattered until there was nothing left but Diane's body, waving like a strip of seaweed or a deboned slice of haddock.

Diane knew she'd succeeded even as the world around her ceased to exist.

A hand grabbed her shoulder and pulled, and another wrapped itself around her midsection, but it wouldn't matter.

She knew she was already gone.

Sunlight touched her cheeks, and the ocean endeavored to take her away.

CHAPTER FORTY-FIVE

MILTY BURKITTS

PLAY ▷

On The Surface

MILTY KICKED HIS FEET, trying desperately to keep his head above the water. Diane was completely limp, the color washed from her face, and a red flower bloomed around the both of them as he treaded frenziedly. The crimson stain followed him as he struggled to drag her lifeless shell to shore and left a long trail behind him once he'd managed to get her back up onto the dock. Exhausted, Milty knelt beside her. He put his lips to hers and gave a couple of quick puffs. Diane's pufferfish cheeks expanded and then relaxed. Expanded and then relaxed. Hands on her chest, he started compressions.

One, two, three, four, stayin' alive, stayin' alive.

He remembered the rhythm and cadence taught to him during his many rounds of CPR training. He'd been a lifeguard at the local YMCA and a card-carrying lifesaver since high school.

Five, six, seven, eight, stayin' alive, stayin' alive.

Her eyes fluttered.

"Diane!" He stopped and put one hand under the back of her head, while his other hand squeezed one of hers tightly. "Diane! Can you hear me?"

She coughed out a swallow of seawater but otherwise didn't respond. Her eyes were still tightly closed, but she was—

"Yes, yes!"

—breathing.

"Hey, hey!" He tapped the back of her hand. "Diane, stay with me! Stay with me!"

The sun was out. A moment before, Milty had made note of how cloudless the sky had become. But, then—as he tried to will a response from Diane—a shadow fell over him. Something was in front of the morning's rays, and it sent a chill racing down his soaking wet spine.

Milty spun around, ready to fight, and—

"Surge?"

The man was already lowering himself down to the ground on the opposite side of Diane's unconscious body. "Uh, yeah. I'm here. But barely." His face was almost entirely red, a deep wound from the top of his forehead actively leaking into his eyes, down his nose, and over his concerned frown. "She's alive too."

Milty nodded, turning his attention back to Diane. "Also barely." He searched their surroundings for a solution but didn't immediately find one. "What do we do?"

In his massive arms, Surge cradled her. As he rose, he groaned. "Thhhere we go." He turned and began to limp back up the dock, toward the parking lot. "Come on. This way. Follow me."

Milty marveled at how the man was still alive, never mind that he still had the strength to carry Diane. "But, where?" Milty said, confused.

Surge, in between gulps of air, nodded at the expanse ahead of them. "Bet your ass there's a phone in the Harbormaster's office."

Milty jogged up ahead. He grabbed the handle of the office door and tugged. "Locked! Now what?"

Surge rolled his eyes and slowly ambled over. Gently, he placed Diane on a wooden bench in the front of the building. "Gimme a second."

Surge put his hands on his hips, breathed in and out a few times, and then roared. He lowered his shoulder and barreled into the door. While it didn't budge on his first attempt, it crashed inward easily on the second.

"Shit, Surge," Milty scratched his head. "How're you—?"

"Ate my Wheaties yesterday. And the day before. And the day before that." He disappeared inside and Milty heard him talking to a dispatcher almost immediately. "Yeah, I'll stay on the line," he said. "But get your asses here fast. She's fading."

Milty leaned over Diane and lifted one of her hands again. Her face was plastered by her wet, blood-infused bangs, and he peeled them away. She was pale—near death, for certain—and he bent over and whispered to her. "Don't know if you can hear me, but they're coming. Help is on the way. You're gonna be okay, Diane."

A wet whistle leaked out from somewhere inside her. Something internally was wrong, and—even though she couldn't speak—her body was trying to let him know.

"You did so great," he said again. "You did it. You *badass*."

A tear trembled near the corner of one of his eyes. Surge was jawing again with the person on the phone, and Milty knew the old man wouldn't be able to hear him.

"So, listen. Next time, we're skipping the bonfire, okay?" he sniffed. "I wanna take you out somewhere *real* special for our second date. How's that sound? I'm thinking somewhere dry, indoors. Maybe...bowling? Candlepin? I bet you'd look cute in those shoes."

Blues and reds and whites flashed from somewhere behind him. Car doors opened and slammed shut. Voices called out, but Milty didn't turn to greet them.

He was staring at Diane.

Her chest had stopped moving.

And nothing more fluttered from underneath her eyelids.

CHAPTER FORTY-SIX

DIANE SHAW

PLAY ▶

Hospital Room

THERE WAS LIGHT THERE. And voices. Muffled and diffused. On the other side. Diane's eyes were closed and heavy, and though she wanted to open them and see what there was to see, even that seemed like something she wasn't quite ready to do. Sleep was a much easier, more appealing balm, and—after everything that'd happened—she felt she'd at least earned the right to rest. And listen. And let everyone else take care of things.

For now. For at least a little bit longer.

Diane had vaguely been aware of her parents in the room. She'd heard the nurses bustling in and out, voices she didn't know but was grateful to have. The song of whatever machine she was hooked up to *beep*ed and *boop*ed, and a couple of other voices she also recognized shuffled in. They both spoke with a relaxed familiarity that suggested this wasn't their first visit—wasn't their first time sitting by her bedside—and she tried, through all the meds and over the quiet drone of a TV left to play on the other side of the room, to hear what they were saying.

"What'd you get?" one of the voices said, a hint of playful ribbing masked by a mouthful of something.

"I'll have you know, this is the finest pile of lettuce money can buy at a beachside burger joint. These leaves have only been wilting for a few days by the look of 'em."

The other laughed again. "Salad? From The Fry Fry? That's a first. Man, you *have* changed."

"Yeah, well. A near-death experience'll do that to ya. Make you suddenly evaluate and consider the simple things. The decisions you were making that maybe you shouldn't have and the ones you weren't but probably should've been." She could sense whoever it was smiling. "Change is a good thing, Son. Change is a good thing. And I'm not complaining."

Surge.

"Well, I get that but...*salad?*"

Milty.

"Don't look at me like that. I need to take care of myself. With business at Bay Video being what it is, I might need to keep on workin' 'til I'm eighty."

Milty took a bite of his meal, serenading her with the melody of his open-mouth chomping. "You make it sound like you actually believe people will still be renting movies from stores decades from now. As if we all won't just have chips implanted in our brains by the year 2000. Mark my words, that's how we'll eventually be watching the great films of our time. All you'll need to do is blink and wham, *Alien*. Blink again and whammo, *Teen Wolf*."

"God, no. Keep that shit outta my head." Diane could hear the crinkling of a plastic container. "VHS is going nowhere. Trust me. Technology will evolve, but that plastic rectangle is *timeless*. How could the viewing experience possibly be improved upon? Besides, I'll be outta business if what you say comes to pass. Nuh uh. No way. You're way, *way* off, Kid." His laugh was a bit hesitant. Diane could tell he didn't fully believe his own words.

There was a long pause, an awkward silence. For a brief moment, Diane wasn't sure what'd happened. But then she heard Milty speaking at a much lower frequency.

"You know," he said. "These docs...they're asking an awful lot of questions."

Surge shifted in his chair. "Mhmm. Police too. Unsurprisingly, they don't believe our story. Not a damn word of it."

"Yeah, well. It doesn't matter, does it? We're *here*."

"That's right. We're here. We made it. Let 'em cover this shit up if that's what they wanna do." A chair squealed. The man must've been standing up. "Let 'em pretend that asshole didn't do what he most certainly did do. Doesn't change a damn thing in the end, does it?"

Milty stood too. Their visit was short, a small window during which Diane's parents had ventured downstairs for a coffee. There were footsteps down the hall, she could hear. They were returning. "No, Surge, it doesn't. Because he's gone for good. He's not comin' back."

Diane felt a hand tap her toes fondly. Another hand brushed some hair from her face. She kept her eyes shut and tried to hide the smile that she worried was growing.

"Bye, Diane," the one nearest her head whispered. "See you tomorrow."

The two men stepped toward the door and she suddenly felt herself unable to resist. She was there. They were there. She'd rested enough. It was time to come back. To get back to the way things were and should be going forward. Diane was ready. Ready to wake up.

"Wait," she said, allowing her eyes to squint open. Both Milty and Surge spun at the sound of her hoarse command, their mouths agape. "Candlepin? *Candlepin*? Is that *really* the best we can do, Milty?"

CHAPTER FORTY-SEVEN

MILTY BURKITTS

PLAY ▷

Bay Video

GLASS CRINKLED. AND CRUNCHED. Milty lifted his foot and tried to avoid stepping directly on any more of the fragments that lay scattered across the floor of the shop.

"Hey, watch where you're walking," Surge called to him from behind the counter. "Last thing we need is you slicing your foot open in those damn Birkenstocks You couldn't have worn sneakers? Or a sturdy pair of boots? This is a major operation here, and you look ready for a day at the goddamn beach."

Milty couldn't help but let out a chuckle. It was his first day back—Surge too—and though there was still so much they needed to do before their planned grand re-opening, he was soaking in just being there. It was a place that'd previously brought so much joy before the tragic, gruesome events that'd occurred a few weeks prior. Milty was ready to move on, as was Surge. And, just as importantly, they were both finally feeling physically ready and able to do the heavy lifting and the grunt work needed to get the place in order so that customers could walk through the door again. Their bodies had healed, for the most part, though the deepest scars—living and breathing in the memories and nightmares that would continue to ooze and bleed, never to coagulate—would live on forever. Milty tensed at the thought and, when Surge tore a strip of duct tape off a piece of cardboard he'd placed over the shattered window, couldn't help but jump a bit at the noise.

"*Jesus*, Surge. Scared me." The older man chuckled as Milty lifted a broom and started sweeping. "And, you know what, my Birks can handle anything. Leave them outta this. Besides, my foot-wrap fits more easily in these."

Surge roared. It was good to hear him laugh so heartily again. While Milty's cuts and bruises were substantial, particularly the sliced Achilles that still had him leaning heavily on a crutch, Surge's wounds had been far more critical. Though he'd carried Diane on that fateful night, he'd nearly collapsed from the loss of blood by the time the paramedics had tended to her. He'd rebounded quickly, far faster than Milty and certainly before Diane, which was an obvious testament to the man's strength and will. "Hah. Well, whatever you say, Son." He paused with the window wide, the storefront temporarily exposed to the chilly November air. A crew would be there later in the day to install the new glass. "I hope you don't take this the wrong way, but—"

"On, no. Here we go. What?"

"—no, no. Hang on. Just listen to me for a minute." He threw the piece of cardboard he'd been gripping to the tile floor. "Don't take this the wrong way, but I hope you don't stay here—with me, in this godforsaken place—for too much longer."

Milty halted his sweeping. He *was* taking it the wrong way. "Um, okay? What're you—are you saying you don't want me here anymore or—?"

Surge stormed over, stepping right into the glass shards on the floor without even pausing. He grabbed Milty by the shoulders and forced him down into a nearby folding chair. Surge sat down in another beside him. "Well, yes. And no. See, I think the world of you, Kid. I really do. And there's no one else I'd want running this place with me now and, hell, taking over after I'm gone, but—"

"Then what's the problem?"

"—I don't want you here forever. What I mean is, I want *more* for you. So much more for you than, well—*this*. All of this." He waved his hands over his head.

Milty folded his arms over his chest protectively. He still wasn't entirely sure where Surge was going with his unexpected proclamation. "But I love this place. What else do I need? Where else do I need to go?"

Surge sighed and leaned back in his chair. "For chrissakes, you idiot. You don't need to work in a goddamn video rental joint until you turn gray. That's my job. You—well, you're destined for *more*. I want *more*. For *you*."

Milty looked around. "Like...*what*?"

Surge groaned. "Do I need to spell it out for you? How 'bout a *life*? How 'bout—well—?"

"What?"

Surge squinted his eyes and leaned forward. "That girl. That woman. You two..."

Diane.

He didn't need to finish the thought. Milty knew what Surge meant. *Who* Surge meant. "I know what you're saying, and—well, I appreciate it. Really. But Diane—if we ever *do* make a go of this, if I ever *do* get that second date—well, she loves Bay Video. Why would she—?"

"She loves *you*, you fool." Surge smiled. "Anyone with half a brain could see that. Except you, apparently."

Milty didn't know what the future held for him or Diane, but he couldn't help but picture one that had both of them in it. Together. And, as far as what Surge was trying to get him to see, he had to acknowledge the possibility that at least part of that could be true. Maybe a life beyond the Bay—Cape Cod *and* Video—would be best. As much of him that was stained on those floors, and as many footprints as they'd both left on those beaches, maybe healing would come faster somewhere else. Maybe a life away—far away—could be what they'd both end up needing. To move on. To fully breathe again.

"Well," Milty blushed. "Don't know about any of that, but—thanks." He slapped the old man on the back. "I promise I'll keep it in mind, though." He rose to his feet and picked up the broom again. "But, for now, this shop—this mess—needs our attention. That's all for later. This," he pointed at the disaster that surrounded them, "is for *now*."

Surge stood and walked back behind the counter. "You're damn right it is. This shit's gonna take us forever if we don't get started." He stepped toward the front entrance and picked up the discarded cardboard. "I'm tossing this out in the dumpster. I'll be right back."

Milty tried to focus on his work as the door slammed behind Surge, but he couldn't help but smile. Surge was right. He would be right back, as would Milty and Diane. In time.

But, for today, Milty thought. *There's a video store that needs a facelift and some tapes that need reshelving.*

He laughed.

These movies aren't gonna watch themselves.

EPILOGUE

1989

PLAY ▷

A Few Months *After*

FEBRUARY WAS A COLD month. Though the creek almost never fully froze over, even on the most frigid of days, there were scattered sheets of snow-covered ice that floated and bobbed along with the ever-moving currents and tides of the Atlantic. Waves rippled against the marina docks, and covered boats sat silent and unoccupied. Even the Harbormaster's light was turned off as the season brought so few to their skiffs.

A shape climbed up and over the dock.

Water dripped, and a puddle formed at the figure's bare feet, but—despite the temperature—the shadow did not tremble or shiver. A layering of black covered the being's extremities, tightly fitting the creature's shape and limbs.

Ziiiiiiiiiiiiip.

It shed its skin and let the husk fall to the wooden panels of the dock. In the moonlight, it held something close to its face: a long, silver-pointed skewer that caught the lunar rays and flicked them back into the eyes of the one who held it so tight.

"A beautiful thing," the iniquitous entity cooed, smiling. It shook the quickly freezing droplets from its long-since-frayed, unkempt dreadlocks. "Such a beautiful, *beautiful* thing."

Rex Templeton tucked the harpoon safely under his arm and calmly walked off, vanishing under and into the wicked shawl of night.

ACKNOWLEDGEMENTS

Thank you to the amazing Shadow Spark Publishing team. To Jessica Moon and Mandy Russell, thank you for believing in my stories and for giving them all (six so far!) a home. To Susan Floyd, who was the first person to read this, and to Azshure Raine, who formatted the hell out of it.

Thank you to Gemma Amor for painting yet another one of my covers. You CRUSHED it.

Thank you to some of my earliest readers—Robert Ottone, Anthony Rapino, and Corey Farrenkopf—whose kind words can be found on the outside of this book.

Thank you to the many friends I have made in the horror community. Getting to be spooky and weird...it's fun, isn't it?

Thank you to the readers who keep reading. Please don't stop.

And most of all, thank you to the three most important people in my life. My three reasons: K.C., A.C., and E.T. Thank you for supporting me and for always allowing me to be myself. I love you all so much.

My children would also probably like me to thank our cat, Binxy Midnight, but I refuse to do so because she is a cat and in no way supported the creation of this book.

Thanks for stopping by yet another of my nightmares. I'll see you in the next one!

Love, Tom

ABOUT THE AUTHOR

Tom Rimer is the author of THE GLOWING Trilogy, MALEVOLENT NEVERS, ODIOUS GHOULS, and BUOYGEIST. His work can also be found in a number of short story anthologies, including 13 Tales to Give You Night Terrors (2015) and The Nightmare Never Ends (2023). He lives in Massachusetts with his family and is a member of the Horror Writers Association.

Find him here:

Website: www.tomrimerauthor.com

Twitter: @RimerTom

Instagram: @Bookishrimer

Goodreads: TomRimer (Author of Malevolent Nevers) (goodreads.com)

Author photo credit: Kacee Rimer

ALSO BY TOM RIMER

Printed in Great Britain
by Amazon

54331316R00117